VILLAINS BY NECESSITY

VILLAINS BY NECESSITY

Sara Woods

We make guilty of our disasters the sun, the
moon, and the stars: as if we were villains by
necessity; fools by heavenly compulsion.

King Lear, Act I, scene ii

St. Martin's Press
New York

First published in Great Britain by Macmillan London Ltd.

Library of Congress Cataloging in Publication Data

Woods, Sara, pseud.
   Villains by necessity.

   I. Title.
PR6073.063V5   1982   823'.914   81-23211
ISBN 0-312-84683-5   AACR2

First Edition

10   9   8   7   6   5   4   3   2   1

PART ONE

Long Vacation, 1973

TUESDAY, September 25th

I

'I don't believe it,' said Antony Maitland flatly, and held the telephone receiver away from his ear as the man at the other end of the line broke into excited expostulation. 'It's all very well, Geoffrey,' he added when he could get a word in, 'Jim's been going straight for years. Seven years,' he added for good measure, after a brief calculation.

'And how many years before that was he a professional crook?' asked Geoffrey Horton bitterly. He was a solicitor, and had no more simple faith in human nature than was proper in a man of his profession. 'He's reverting to type, that's all.'

'What is he supposed to have done?'

'He's been up to his old tricks . . . burglary.'

'And you say he's under arrest?'

'That's exactly what I've been trying to tell you for the last five minutes,' said Geoffrey rather testily. 'The Magistrate's Court hearing was this morning, but he insists he won't have anybody but you when the trial comes on.'

'The police think they've identified his *modus operandi*,' said Maitland, as though inspiration had suddenly struck him.

'I'm afraid that won't wash. If you'd only listen, Antony.'

'I'm listening.'

'He was caught in the flat of a couple called Franklin —'

'Breaking and entering,' said Maitland, interrupting.

'Nothing of the sort. He was caught in the act of leaving, and he'd already possessed himself of a rather valuable collection of coins belonging to Henry Franklin.'

'I see.' Maitland was silent for a moment. 'There's no doubt about it then, he's reverted to type, as you say. Perhaps if Martha hadn't died —'

'Martha was his wife, wasn't she? I'd no idea she was dead. Look

7

here, Antony, are you telling me you've been in touch with him all this time?'

'On and off,' said Maitland, immediately becoming vague.

'Well, perhaps we can use that,' said Geoffrey hopefully. 'If she died recently, we could say he was suffering from shock.'

'I'm afraid that won't wash either, it's three years ago now. I don't think even the most tender hearted jury would believe that a state of shock would last all that time.'

'You said yourself –' Geoffrey began to argue.

'Yes, I know I did. But I didn't mean exactly that, only that I know she was very keen on his going straight, and I think she had a good deal of influence over him.'

It was Geoffrey's turn to say, 'I see. He tells me he's been running a little shop since he came out, one his wife started while he was inside,' he went on.

'Stationery and tobacco,' said Maitland precisely. He hesitated a moment. 'Uncle Nick bought it for her,' he said.

'But Sir Nicholas had never anything to do with the Arnolds,' said Geoffrey, becoming argumentative again. 'We defended him several times, but –'

'Do you remember the last time?'

'In the early 'sixties, wasn't it?'

'Late nineteen sixty-one.'

'How on earth do you remember so exactly?'

'I have my reasons. It's your turn to listen, Geoffrey. Do you remember that at that time we thought we could get him off with a lighter sentence if only he'd tell us what he'd done with the stolen goods? And when he wouldn't we came to two conclusions. First that he'd already disposed of the doings and that he was dead scared to talk. And secondly that he was expecting some sort of a pension when he got out again.'

'I remember those were *your* ideas.'

'Don't be so stuffy, Geoffrey, I say that was true. The next thing is, do you remember Jo Marston?'

'Is she the sort of person you'd forget?' Geoffrey asked rhetorically.

'No, I don't think so. In that case you'll also remember that in trying to clear Roy Bromley –'

8

'In which we weren't altogether successful.'

'– she succeeded in getting herself kidnapped.'

'I also remember that you told me nothing about that until it was all over,' said Geoffrey rather bitterly.

'There was a reason for that. I'd already decided that the matter we were investigating would tie in somehow with the same gang Jim Arnold had been working for, but I promised Martha faithfully I wouldn't say a word to anybody, that was the only reason I wasn't frank with you at the time.'

'What on earth has Martha Arnold got to do with it?'

'She was able to help me in getting Jo released, I mean in telling me of a place where she might possibly be. And as it turned out she was right.'

'But why should Sir Nicholas set her up in business because of that?'

'Don't you see, her action closed the door on Jim's pension. Jo was kidnapped in place of Jenny, so that Uncle Nick and I had a special reason to be grateful for her release. The shop was intended to be a going concern by the time Jim came out of prison, a new way of life for him, a chance to turn over a new leaf.'

'When did he come out?'

'He got full remission, as I remember, and came out some time in nineteen sixty six. I don't recall exactly when. To tell you the truth I haven't seen much of him since Martha died, which was about three years ago. She had cancer.'

'I expect you were right, that it was the removal of her influence that sent Jim back to his old ways again. Anyway, you do see now, Antony – don't you? – that there's no doubt about his guilt and all we can do is put the best complexion we can on his reasons.'

'You reserved his defence, of course?'

'Of course.'

'Well, what did he tell you about his reasons?'

'Not much,' Geoffrey admitted. 'I think, to tell you the truth, he may be more frank with you.'

'As to that, who lives may learn. Was he in financial straits? Was the shop doing badly? If that's the case he's more of a fool than ever, he could have come to me.'

'Once a thief always a thief. He followed his natural instinct,'

9

said Geoffrey didactically. 'And if he wanted to retire, he's just started to draw his old age pension. He could have sold the shop and been quite comfortably off I should think.'

'Of all the little rays of sunshine!' said Antony, and in spite of himself a note of amusement had crept into his voice. 'You're telling me we haven't got a defence at all.'

'You'll think of something.'

'I'm glad you have so much faith in my ingenuity.'

'You will take the case?' asked Horton anxiously.

'Oh yes, I suppose I must. For old time's sake if for no other reason. Did you get him bail?'

'No, the police were rather sticky about that. I suppose one can't blame them, considering his past record. I know you hate it, Antony, but I'm afraid we shall have to go out to Brixton to see him.'

'So be it. When do you want to go?' He was pulling his calendar towards him as he spoke.

'As soon as possible I should think, to get it over with,' said Geoffrey. 'It won't take much of your time, this is one case where there's no point in pleading Not Guilty, except to give you a chance to put in a plea in extenuation.'

'Where no extenuating circumstances exist,' said Antony, though he did not sound unduly cast down. 'Would ten o'clock tomorrow morning suit you, Geoffrey, can you arrange it for then?'

'That will be fine, I'll call for you at home, shall I? And, of course,' he added rather perfunctorily – for they were old friends these two – 'I'll be sending the papers over to Mallory.'

'Thank you. Why not come a bit early, and have a cup of coffee with us before we set out?'

'Good idea,' said Geoffrey, and rang off without further ado. But Maitland was thoughtful as he turned his attention again to the pile of documents that had accumulated during the long vacation, and though he succeeded in banishing Jim Arnold's problems from his mind while he dealt with the more urgent of them, those problems came back to him very forcibly when he left chambers a little later than usual to make his way home.

Antony Maitland and his wife, Jenny, had their own quarters at the top of Sir Nicholas Harding's house in Kempenfeldt Square, which Antony – except when he was exceptionally late or exceptionally tired – regarded as being an easy walk from chambers. Sir Nicholas was Antony's uncle and, with his wife Vera, occupied the main part of the house. The arrangement had been made 'temporarily' many years before, but it was a long time since any of them had thought of it in that way; though it must be admitted that Antony had known some scruples after his uncle's marriage, not much more than two years before, as to whether he and Jenny might not be in the way. However, these doubts had been banished very quickly to everyone's satisfaction, the traditions between the two households that had grown up over the years had been resumed, and even if they had not loved her for herself both Antony and Jenny would have had to agree that the new Lady Harding was a distinct acquisition

Sir Nicholas, a man inclined to be autocratic with his nearest and dearest, was paradoxically the sort of person who is at the mercy of his servants. Even Gibbs, the ancient butler who refused to retire, seemed to regard Vera with favour. In many ways he was as intransigent as ever, and certainly just as disapproving of his employer's nephew, whom he still seemed to regard as the boy of thirteen who had first joined the household; but he had – concession of concessions! – finally agreed to use the house phone to announce visitors for the upstairs quarters, instead of stumping up to do so in person, which was distressing even though everybody knew he enjoyed his martyrdom.

There was a further link between Maitland and his uncle besides their relationship. Both were Queens Counsel, and Sir Nicholas was head of the chambers in the Inner Temple to which his nephew belonged. This was an undoubted convenience when there were matters to be argued over, and as Vera too had been a barrister until her marriage, though in the junior branch of the profession and on a different circuit, she enjoyed the legal shop as much as anybody. As for Jenny, she was a gentle soul, a better listener than a talker on the whole, but after so many years she was capable of taking a really intelligent interest in every matter that came under advisement.

That evening, being Tuesday, the Hardings were dining upstairs. That was the evening that Mrs Stokes, Sir Nicholas's housekeeper, chose to take herself to the pictures, and her employer had consequently been a fugitive for many years from the cold collation which she had been accustomed to leave him. Jenny suspected that Vera would have been glad enough to take possession of the kitchen occasionally, but even with her beneficial influence over the household they all realised it was quite impossible.

Sir Nicholas had returned from chambers at his usual time that evening, and he and Vera were already with Jenny in the big, comfortable, but rather shabby living-room. That was something else Antony and Jenny had always meant to change, the assortment of furniture that each of them had inherited from their own side of the family, so that the only matching things in the whole room were the two wing chairs that flanked the fireplace. Everybody admitted that the sofa was hideous, and Jenny sometimes reminded Sir Nicholas – who never sat on it – that it had only been given house room at his particular request. On these occasions he would give his most benign smile, and assure her that she was perfectly at liberty to dispose of it in any way she wished. But by then she had become accustomed to its comfort, had taken over the corner nearest the windows as her special place, and somehow she never got round to availing herself of this permission.

When Antony went in, an argument was going on between Sir Nicholas and Jenny as to whether, considering the coolness of the evening, a match should be put to the fire. Vera, who was known to feel the heat when there was any, was keeping very carefully on the sidelines, until at last appealed to by both parties she cast her vote in favour of the fire. 'The first fire of winter,' she said comfortably, settling herself well back in the corner of the sofa nearest her husband's favourite chair. 'Or have you had to have one before?'

'No, that's just as I left it in the spring,' said Jenny. 'Are you sure, Vera?'

'Quite sure,' Vera assured her. 'There's nothing quite like sitting

12

round an open fire.' But Jenny was still looking doubtful when Antony, having greeted the others, stepped past her, appropriated the box of Swan Vestas from the table at his uncle's elbow, and knelt down in front of the grate to coax the fire into a blaze, which he thought might take some doing on a cold hearth.

Jenny went to fetch him some sherry – the rest of them were already provided – and knowing his habits placed it on the mantel-piece near the clock. Antony concentrated for the moment on what he was doing. At the end of the long vacation, and with nothing on his conscience at the moment to which he thought Sir Nicholas could take exception, he was looking forward to an account of his uncle and aunt's travels on the continent, and to recounting himself certain select episodes that had occurred during their summer in the country. But it was not to be, not yet at any rate. While he was still watching anxiously for the first flicker of flame his uncle remarked, in the cordial tone that he knew only too well might spell trouble, 'Mallory tells me you had a long tele-phone conversation with Geoffrey Horton this afternoon.'

That simple remark had the immediate effect of diverting Antony's attention. 'Mallory should mind his own business,' he said rather hotly.

'He's my clerk,' said Sir Nicholas, 'so it's very much his business what goes on in chambers. No papers have been received from Geoffrey's firm, and if you're going to tell me it was a personal matter may I remind you that I've never yet known him phone chambers for such a cause.'

'Of course I'm not going to tell you that,' said Antony. He turned to look at the fire again and was encouraged by what he saw. 'You know perfectly well Joan and Jenny arrange everything of a social nature between them. This was work, the brief will be along in due course, he just wanted to know if I'd accept it.'

'Knowing the kind of cases Geoffrey takes some interest in –'

'Well, this is quite a simple one, nothing out of the way. An old client of mine,' said Antony. 'And come to think of it you may be interested in that, Uncle Nick. It's Jim Arnold.' He scrambled to his feet as he spoke and retrieved his sherry, retreating thereafter to the chair opposite his uncle's.

Sir Nicholas meanwhile had put down his own glass with exaggerated care and was sitting bolt upright, glaring across at his nephew. 'Jim Arnold?' he said incredulously. And then, forgetting his surprise for a moment to assume an accusing tone, 'I seem to remember, Antony, your recommending him to me as a deserving case.'

'Nothing of the sort.' Jenny was up in arms immediately. 'It was your own idea, Uncle Nick, I remember it perfectly.'

Vera looked from one to the other of her assembled family with a rather grim smile. She was a tall woman with a pleasant contralto voice, and very thick greying hair that was always on the verge of escaping from the confining pins, especially when anything excited her. 'Got to remember, Nicholas,' she said now in her gruff way, 'I haven't the faintest idea what you're talking about.'

'I must apologise, my dear, though I expect I've told you about the affair at some time or another. One of Antony's more mismanaged cases,' he added.

'He didn't mismanage it at all,' said Jenny rebelliously.

'I don't know what else you'd call it,' said Sir Nicholas reflectively. 'To be brief, Vera, things got into such a tangle that Antony had to rely on the help of the wife of one of his clients in sorting them out. The client, I might add, was a confirmed criminal, at that time serving a sentence of – what was it, Antony? – five years, I believe.' 'Still don't understand,' said Vera.

'Jim Arnold was involved with a . . . may I say "gang", Uncle Nick?' Antony took up the story. 'It sounds rather melodramatic, but I can't think of any other way of putting it.'

'If you wish,' said Sir Nicholas, sighing and leaning back in his chair again as though things were getting too much for him.

'What I'm trying to tell you, Vera,' said Antony, 'is that he could have expected what I can only call a pension when he came out of stir.' His attention was ostensibly on his aunt, but he was noting his uncle's reaction at the same time. Sir Nicholas, who affected an extreme aversion to slang when anyone but Vera used it, now closed his eyes in a pained way and appeared to swoon. 'So when Mrs Arnold gave me the information that helped to clear up the whole matter she was doing her husband and family an extreme disservice. That was why Uncle Nick came to the rescue and bought a small shop for them. Martha Arnold ran it until Jim came out, and then he took over. I was in touch with them until the time she died, three years or so ago. She was very keen on his going straight, but I dare say now he's on his own again ... well, I haven't heard his story yet, but I gather he was caught on some- one's premises with the loot on him.'

'What sort of loot?' asked Vera who had a practical mind.

'A collection of coins. I didn't get much information from Geoffrey really, he said Jim was unwilling to talk to anyone but me.'

'If the matter is as clear cut as all that,' said Sir Nicholas, 'there's no need for you to see him at all.'

'Oh, I think there is.' Antony took refuge in vagueness. 'Call it for old time's sake if you like. Anyway, I must admit to a certain curiosity.'

'You don't think,' said Jenny hesitantly, 'that he's got mixed up with another gang?'

Antony turned and smiled at her. 'I don't think that at all, love,' he said. 'I think it was probably just boredom. Anyway, as Uncle Nick says, it's quite clear cut, and all I have to do is try and find something to say in extenuation.'

'From the sound of it,' said Sir Nicholas, 'that will be rather diffi- cult.' He had come to life again and was sipping his sherry, a man with an unconscious air of authority about him, who had always been very fair so that now the increasing number of white hairs scarcely showed. He and his nephew were both tall men though Sir Nicholas was far more heavily built, and there was, oddly enough, an elusive likeness between them ... odd because they were so very dissimilar in feature. The newspapers had been known to call Sir Nicholas handsome, on which occasions the female members of the household conspired together to keep the offending edition out of his sight. No-one had ever been known to refer to Maitland in that way, and he was, besides, as dark as his uncle was fair. He had a preference for the casual, severely sub- dued in his professional life, with a gift for mimicry which in general he used quite unconsciously, and rather more sense of humour than was sometimes good for him.

'I can quite see it's no use talking to you,' said Sir Nicholas now.

'You'll go your own way whatever I say.' Vera and Jenny exchanged a smile at that, knowing well enough that he wouldn't have had it any other way. 'Well, that's all very satisfactory,' the older man went on with one of his bewildering changes of mood. 'I never met this man, Arnold, but I remember being very impressed with his wife.'

'She was a good soul,' Antony agreed. He put down his empty glass wondering – again rather vaguely – how it had happened to get that way. 'Shall I do the honours, or will you, Jenny?' he asked. 'Personally I find getting back into harness again quite exhausting.'

After which it was, of course, a foregone conclusion that Jenny should get up and circulate the decanter.

III

'It got better,' said Jenny, when they were alone at last and she was rounding up the brandy glasses, 'but what was the matter with Uncle Nick? He was like that when he arrived.'

'Like what, love?' Antony asked idly, but he smiled as he spoke. People generally did smile at Jenny.

'Like a cat with its fur rubbed the wrong way. And then about Jim Arnold. It isn't as if you're going to get involved with any-thing . . . or is it?' she added anxiously.

'A simple defence, Jenny love, you can forget the gang,' her husband assured her.

'Well, that's what I thought, but what *was* the matter with him?'

'He's had a bad day, I expect. You know it isn't easy picking up the threads after the long vacation.' He paused and grinned as a thought occurred to him. 'As a matter of fact I looked into his room as I left this evening in case he was still there. Well, you know how Mallory arranges everything so neatly for him to come back to.'

'Yes, you've told me.'

'He'd already reduced the whole surface of his desk to a state of utter chaos. It will stay that way too unless I do something about it. It's odd, Jenny, because you know what he's like, he really hates untidiness but he can't work any other way.'

'Well, at least,' said Jenny putting down the tray on the table by the door and coming back to the fireside again, 'he's got it out of his system. Now he knows there's nothing out of the way about this new client —'

'This old client,' Antony corrected her. 'I can't help feeling sorry about it though. I really thought Jim was going straight at last.'

I

The next morning was sunny, though still on the cold side. Maitland, seated beside Horton in the big car that was the solici- tor's pride and joy even though it was growing rather elderly now, huddled his coat about him as though the temperature were far lower than it actually was. 'It's time you got over it, Antony,' Horton told him briskly. He seemed in a buoyant mood this morning, for in the normal way he would never have deliberately ventured a remark calculated to arouse the worst in his companion, and whose effect he knew well enough beforehand.

'Get over what?' asked Maitland disagreeably.

'This phobia you have about prison visiting.'

'Let's leave my feelings out of it, shall we? A dismal business, that's all there's to it.' It was ridiculous, he knew, to shy away from all discussion of the subject, the horror that gripped him on his way to the interview room as each grille in turn clanged shut and was locked behind him, was real enough; but there was only one person in the world to whom he would willingly speak of this, or of the injury to his shoulder which still after so many years gave him considerable pain. It wasn't Sir Nicholas (though once he had been reasonably frank with his uncle, more or less under duress); it wasn't even Jenny – he'd hurt her in the past, he knew, however unwittingly, and he shrank from doing so further, even while he was perfectly well aware that she of all people knew him through and through. But for the moment there was Geoffrey to cope with, a good friend who had stood behind him time and again when the going was rough. 'I didn't mean to be a grouch,' he said aloud.

'My fault,' said Geoffrey, almost as gruffly as Vera might have done. But he'd evidently not quite recovered from his attack of candour. 'It's only . . . you've got to realise it gives your friends no pleasure at all to see you torture yourself.'

Antony laughed suddenly, the humour that was never very far below the surface of his thoughts suddenly getting the better of his annoyance at being reminded of the past. 'Exaggeration from you, Geoffrey?' he said, almost lightly. 'That won't do. If you aren't around to keep my feet on the ground, where shall I be?'

'In trouble again,' said Geoffrey, who had a literal mind. 'But look here, Antony, this morning's errand is nothing to worry about. Jim Arnold's going back to prison, there's nothing we can do about that, and it isn't as if it will be a new experience for him. He's been in and out of jail all his life.'

'You're right, of course. All the same, as I told you, I do feel a certain responsibility towards Mrs Arnold.'

'Who is dead,' Geoffrey reminded him.

'Let's put it another way then. Towards what she would have wished for her husband.'

'It isn't your fault he forsook the straight and narrow,' said Geoffrey bluntly.

'Of course it isn't. All the same –' He let the sentence trail into silence. 'I think perhaps I ought to have kept in touch with him,' he added after a while.

'That's nonsense,' Geoffrey told him roundly. Then he smiled in his turn. 'However, I have to admit you're in exactly the frame of mind our client must have wished.'

'What do you mean by that?'

'He wouldn't talk to me and I didn't press him because there wasn't really any need at that stage. But if he's going to tell you a sob story you're in just the mood to take it in lock, stock and barrel, and put it over to the jury in due course.'

'*I am no orator as Brutus is*,' said Maitland, again striving for a lighter tone.

'No,' said Horton seriously, and Antony laughed aloud.

'There's nothing like having a candid friend for keeping one from getting a swelled head,' he remarked.

'What I meant,' said Geoffrey carefully, 'is that I think your strength lies in believing what you say, and getting that fact over to the court.'

'You'd better quit while you're ahead,' Maitland advised him. But he remained thoughtful, and wasn't to be tempted into any

19

further conversation until they arrived at the prison.

Jim Arnold had really changed very little in the years since Maitland had seen him, the same rather ineffectual looking little man, very neat in a blue serge suit that might well be the same one he had been wearing on his last appearance in court. That ineffectual air had stood him in good stead in the past with people who didn't know him well; unfortunately the police could not be counted among their number.

'I take this very kindly in you, I do indeed, Mr Maitland,' he said as soon as the warder had left the three of them alone together in the interview room. 'But there wasn't really no need.'

'As you wouldn't talk to Mr Horton I think there was every need. It's a clear case —'

'Now Mr Maitland, would I do a thing like that?'

'Yes, Jim, you would,' said Maitland with brutal frankness.

'Martha wouldn't like to hear you say that,' said Jim reproach-fully.

'Perhaps if Martha was still alive it wouldn't have happened. Come now, Jim, you've got to tell me why you did it. I've got to have something to say in extenuation.'

'I was drunk,' said Jim. 'I'm ashamed to say I was drunk.' Any shame he actually felt was certainly well concealed. 'And when I came to meself I found meself in this chap's flat.'

'On enclosed premises,' said Maitland inexorably.

'That's right guv'nor, but you see it wasn't my fault. So I was just having a look round as anybody would, and I just got my hands on these coins — a silly hobby if you ask me — when out he pops from the bedroom, and his wife at his heels. Well I hadn't no idea of taking nothing, just an accident I was there at all. But you know what people are guv, always think the worst.'

'Can you blame them? What about the tools of your trade?'

'House-breaking implements would sound more classy,' Jim pointed out reprovingly. 'Well, I did have a set of twirls on me — how else would I have got into the place, even by accident? — but I only carry those for old times sake, like.'

Maitland looked at him for a long moment. 'All right, Jim, let's have done with the fairy tales,' he urged. 'Tell me the truth now.'

'But, Mr Maitland —'

'The truth,' said Antony. 'And I may add, Jim, that I'm not particularly flattered that you thought I might fall for this story of yours, when you hadn't even the face to tell it to Mr Horton.'

'You really think it won't wash?' said Jim, for the first time show-ing some signs of despondency.

'Of course it won't!' He got up from his chair as he spoke and began to pace the width of the narrow room. Then a thought struck him and he whirled round to face Horton. 'I didn't ask you, Geoffrey, and perhaps I should have done. It wasn't aggravated burglary?'

'No no, nothing like that,' said Jim Arnold soothingly before his solicitor had time to answer. 'Would I do a thing like that?' he asked again.

'Carry a firearm? No, I have to admit it wouldn't be like you,' said Maitland. 'But this whole thing . . . you swore you were going straight after the last time.'

'If I hadn't got so drunk –'

'I don't believe that either. Where did this orgy take place anyway?'

'That's something I can't remember, any more than I can remember how I got into this Mr Franklin's flat.'

'Oh, what's the use!' He went back to his chair and stood behind it, his hands gripping the wooden rail at the back. 'I don't believe you, Jim, and the court certainly won't believe either of us if I present them with this rigmarole. If you can't think of anything better –'

'You're not telling me you'd leave me in the lurch, Mr Maitland,' said Jim, reproachful again.

'That's exactly what I'm telling you. From what Mr Horton tells me that collection of coins was extremely valuable. Why did you want the money? Is the business doing badly?'

'Well you know yourself, guv'nor, a lot of people have given up smoking.'

'Yes, but the prices have gone up.'

'Government takes most of that.'

'But not all of it, Jim. Besides, it isn't exclusively a tobacconist's shop, there are the newspapers too and the magazines.'

'Well, I admit I was doing well enough. It's closed up now, of course.'

'Wasn't there anyone to look after it for you? Jimmy . . . I expect he's got a good job in his own line by now, but what about Doris?'

'Didn't you know, guv, they're both in Canada?'

'No, I didn't know that.'

'Got the idea into their heads and went after Martha died. Well, of course, the arrangements aren't made in a minute, about two and a half years ago it was when they left. They're both married now.'

'I was still thinking of them as children,' Maitland admitted.

'Jimmy's twenty-nine, got a good job near Toronto, one of the big engineering firms. Doris's husband is a mate of his. She's been working in a dress shop, boutique they calls them now, but she's expecting so I don't suppose she'll be there very much longer.' He stopped there and held up a hand when Antony started to speak. 'No, wait a bit, guv,' he said. 'I had an idea but it takes a bit of thinking about.'

'Another lie I suppose,' said Antony sceptically.

'Not a bit of it. You see, Mr Maitland,' said Jim with a disarming air of candour, 'they wants me to go out there and join them, well not to live with them, I wouldn't do that, but somewhere near. And it gets lonely like without Martha. I'd need my fare money and it sounds better when you make your application if you've got a bit behind you.'

'It never occurred to you, I suppose, that the immigration authorities in Canada might not look with all that favour on an old lag?'

'That's not a nice way of putting it, Mr Maitland,' said Jim reprovingly. 'As for the past, I wouldn't have to tell them every-thing, would I now?'

'You mean you'd deliberately lie on your application form?'

'If you was a Jesuit father now, you wouldn't be asking me a thing like that and sounding so shocked,' said Jim.

'Why ever not?' asked Maitland, rather startled.

'Something about not having to tell the truth if the chap asking the questions doesn't expect you to,' Jim told him vaguely.

'I can't help feeling you've got that wrong. In any case I'm not a Jesuit father,' Antony objected, and added smiling, 'I've a feeling the superior general might frown on my – my marital arrange-ments.'

22

'Yes, how is Mrs Maitland?' demanded Jim, obviously snatching at the chance of changing the subject.

'She's very well and we'll stick to your affairs if you please. You want to go to Canada, and you need your fare and a certain amount of capital in addition to your pension to induce the powers that be to look kindly upon your application. Have I got that right?'

'Absolutely guv'nor.'

'Is that the truth?'

'Cross my heart,' Jim asserted.

'Then it leads to another question, and don't think I'm the only person who'll ask it if I bring all this up in court. Why not sell the shop?'

'I'm getting on in years,' said Jim pathetically. 'I just didn't want the delay.'

'A term in prison will delay you still longer,' Maitland pointed out. 'Come on now, the real reason.'

'We don't have to tell them about the shop.'

'Do you think the police don't know already? Of course they do. I will *not* go into court with half a story,' said Antony firmly.

'Haven't changed at all, have you?' Jim grumbled. 'You always was a disbelieving sort of bloke. All right then, I didn't put the shop up for sale because I daren't.'

'You're telling me you're connected with organized crime again?'

'Nothing of the kind, guv'nor. Not the way you means. I've been paying protection,' said Jim.

Antony and Geoffrey exchanged a despairing glance. 'Why the hell didn't you tell me this before?' Maitland demanded.

'Do you think it makes a better story?' asked Jim, surprised.

'Of course it does! If it's true,' he added as a sudden doubt assailed him. But somehow now he had a feeling . . .

'It's true all right,' Jim asserted.

'Then tell me the whole thing. Who's involved and how long it's been going on.'

'I'll begin at the beginning,' said Jim. 'Which really is when I came out the last time, and you know, Mr Maitland, it was a bit of a facer what had been happening while I was inside. But there was you and Sir Nicholas and you'd been good to Martha, and there

23

was a nice little business all waiting for me to take over. Which I did.'

'That was about seven years ago, wasn't it?'

'Yes it was, and all went like a breeze for the first couple of years. That is when it started, five years ago. They wanted money, they wanted it regular, and they knew to a penny how much I could afford and still live. I suppose it didn't suit them to make their clients desperate, but you only had to look at what happened to them as didn't pay to make you pretty scared not to. All the same it meant we weren't saving a penny.'

'What happened to the people who didn't pay? I suppose you mean to other shopkeepers in the neighbourhood?'

'Only one as I knows on, but it stands to reason there'd be others. And it was the usual thing, he'd been beaten up and the place wrecked. It didn't pay you to argue,' said Jim almost philoso-phically.

'Did your family know about this?'

'Not on your life. Jimmy and Doris was home then, and even what they brought in was allowed for, in estimating what we could live on. I had to tell them what I told Martha, that the shop was doing badly. She never said a word but I know she thought perhaps it was my fault, because it had been doing all right while she was running it. And she offered to come back, I had to play the heavy husband and absolutely forbid it. She was a proper woman and would always do what I said.'

'She was indeed,' Maitland agreed. 'And you're still paying, or rather you were until you got in here?'

'Well, you know, guv'nor, I didn't really like the position,' said Jim thoughtfully. 'But when you've got hostages to fortune, as they say, there's nothing much you can do about a thing like that.'

'You're telling me the threats included them?'

'A'course they did. What do you expect? Only after Martha died –'

'You suggested to the children that they go to Canada,' said Antony.

'Yes, I did.' For some reason Jim sounded almost defiant. 'Get them out of harm's way, that's what I thought, then perhaps I could do something about it.'

'What for instance?'

'Do you really want to know?'

'Why do you think I'm asking?'

'There was two of them as made the collections. I don't know how many districts they covered, but in Fulham it was always on a Monday they came, the first Monday of the month. I don't know who else they called on either, except the chap I told you about as got beaten up, but I had to wait until a day they came late, just as I was putting up the shutters. Then I paid up all innocent like, but when they left I followed.'

'That was rather a risky thing to do, wasn't it?'

'I'd only myself to worry about by then, and . . . well to tell you the truth, guv'nor, it riled me, paying them off like that. If they'd had a car I'd have been sunk, I haven't got one and couldn't afford it with all they took off me. But they set off on foot right across the Fulham Road and down to Parsons Green tube station. That was enough for one night I thought, so I scarpered.'

'It can't have been easy shadowing two men who knew you well.'

'It wasn't, that's what I'm telling you. Well, I figured it out that probably they covered their route in a different direction on different days, but probably finished up about the same time. So the next time they were due –'

'Wait a bit! They didn't come every week then?'

'No, didn't I say? The first Monday of every month.'

'So you did. I'd forgotten for the moment.'

'Anyway, I'm telling you, the next time they came to me quite early on, so I shut up the shop in good time and went down to Parsons Green. I'd worked it out they were probably going North to change at Earls Court and finish up somewhere in the West End, and I missed them altogether that evening. A month later I tried the southbound platform, reading my newspaper while I waited as anyone might, and that time I spotted them and got on the train, though not of course in the same carriage.'

'Of course not,' Antony agreed, quite fascinated by now with this saga.

'And they got off at Wimbledon Park,' said Jim impressively. He was warming to his story now, perhaps encouraged by his listeners' obvious interest.

'Still together?'

'Oh yes, I wondered about that too, but I got it worked out that perhaps those were instructions. Whoever was organising the affair didn't trust either of them alone. Anyway I saw them get off at Wimbledon Park, but again I didn't try and follow. I just went on to the end of the line and back home again. And after that I let it go for a month or two. Not that I lost my nerve or anything like that, but I thought it was time to think things over. And then I chanced my arm and closed early Wednesday, and went down to Wimbledon Park and hung around in the station. I was wearing dark glasses and a cloth cap pulled down over my eyes, and I thought that not being their Fulham day they wouldn't be expect-ing to see me. Of course, I kept out of sight as well as I could too, the old newspaper trick like I said before.'

'Did they come?'

'They came all right, about half an hour later than I'd expected them though. Wherever they'd been it had been a longer journey, I suppose. But they didn't see me, and when they left I shoved the paper in my pocket and followed. That wasn't so difficult, they didn't suspect nothing.'

'Where did they lead you?'

'Eastwards, well, north-east really. Across Durnsford Road and past the power station, almost into Earlsfield.'

'You seem to know that area very well.'

'Bless you guv'nor, I've done jobs all round there, and other places as well, you'd be surprised. Anyway they knew where they were going all right, a very small block of flats called Kenyon Court. I didn't know it then but there are just four flats altogether, rather large ones. I watched these two go in and then I went home.'

'So you've no idea what their business was there?'

'Well, it was obvious wasn't it? Not the type to be living in a swell place like that.'

'You'd better tell me a little more about these two men.'

'I don't know their full names, only that they call each other Alf and Stan sometimes.'

'Incautious of them.'

'Not really, they'd think I'd be too scared to try to find out who they were.'

'Did they ever say anything to you, Jim, to indicate that they knew your record?'

'Oh they knew all right, that was one of the things that scared me in the first place. They said anything Drayton could have done they'd do a hundred times over if I didn't play ball.'

'Could they have been part of that outfit?'

'Could 'a'been. I didn't know all –'

'All your fellow workers,' Maitland concluded for him. 'You were taking a risk, weren't you, even though those hostages to fortune you spoke of weren't around any longer?'

'I told you, they riled me.'

It was at this point that Geoffrey entered the conversation. Knowing his friend, he'd been quite content to allow him his head, but this was something that Maitland ought to know. 'As I remember, Jim, it was one of the flats at Kenyon Court that you're accused of burgling.'

'That's right guv'nor. I told you I was a reformed character. Trying to get me own back, that's all I was doing.'

'You're saying that this Henry Franklin was the man who set Alf and Stan on to collecting money from you?'

'Well, I don't know,' said Jim with an air of frankness. 'Those two didn't live there, that was pretty certain, rough types, not at all the sort a posh place like that would have been rented to. So I thought the man behind it all must be one of the four tenants, and I'd do my best to find out which it was.'

'How did you set about that?' Geoffrey asked.

'I went back on Sunday when the shop was shut. Not just one Sunday, of course, but week after week after week. And I found out this and that about the people who live there.'

'Just a moment, Jim.' Antony interrupted again. 'You said four flats, how were they arranged?'

'Two on each floor. I went in, felt safe enough doing that, because of course the man I was after didn't know anything about me except the colour of my money. There was a widish hall, and a door on each side, number one on the right, number two on the left, no lift but a flight of shallow stairs going up to the first floor,

27

same arrangement there only the flats were numbered three and four.'

'When you watched from the outside was there nothing to indicate which one the men had gone to? Light switched on, anything like that?'

'Not a thing, guv'nor. The lights in the hallways were on anyway, and at that time of the evening –'

'Yes, what time was it?'

'About seven-thirty to eight o'clock. At that time all of the flats had a light in what I took to be the living-room, and some of them other lights beside. There was nothing whatever to tell which one Alf and Stan had gone to, though I went back again several times at around that same hour in the evening and watched them go in. But I kept well out of the way, you can be sure of that.'

'They were regular visitors then?'

'Every evening during the week so far as I could tell.'

'You were going to tell us something about the tenants of Kenyon Court.'

'Well this Henry Franklin isn't a tenant really, he owns the place. I didn't get all this information at once you know, guv'nor, I had to go back as I told you, didn't want to arouse any suspicions. And you see the only day I had free was Sunday, when I couldn't follow any of them to their place of business or anything like that. But I got friendly with the chap in the little shop on the corner who stays open on a Sunday . . . which is a thing I'd never do,' he added righteously. 'Sometimes he'd leave his missus in charge and come along with me to the pub when it opened, and I told him a tale of having known someone who'd lived just where Kenyon Court is now, only they'd been bombed out. That made it natural like, for me to be interested in the new place.'

'All right then, what did you learn from all these researches?'

'Mr Franklin owned the place. Well, he might be joint owner with his wife, I wouldn't know about that. He's sixtyish but retired already, owned an antique shop and made his pile early from what I heard. Which isn't so unlikely as it sounds, guv'nor, if you take my meaning. There's people as pay good money for all kinds of trash.'

'So I believe. And his wife?'

'If she ever had an occupation she'd retired too. But if you ask

28

me there'd have been nothing like that. No need, if you take my meaning.'

'I see. And the rest of the people who lived there? The tenants?'

'Flat One on the ground floor is occupied by some people called Prior, and there are two couples upstairs, the Dickinsons and the Shelleys.'

'Did you learn no more than their names?'

'Now then, guv'nor, I've been haunting the place for months,' Jim protested. 'A course I learned more than that. Not much more,' he added thoughtfully, 'but something.'

'Tell me, then.'

'Well, I told you about the Franklins.'

'Not much.'

'All I know. And the other people on the ground floor, the Priors. He's a civil engineer which means he's away from home a lot, I understand, and she was Henry Franklin's assistant at the shop, and now manages the place for the new owner. I suppose she gets bored, her husband being away from home so much.'

'And the people upstairs?'

'Well, I tell you frankly, there's most talk about Mrs Dickinson. She's not well liked in the district. An American,' he added.

'Come now, that's not sufficient reason for disliking her,' said Antony, his mind going at once to Sam Henderson whom once he had known very well but hadn't seen now for something like seven years. A good chap to have on your side when the going was tough.

'No, but it's not a reason for liking her either, not when she throws her weight about as it seems she does. She's a doctor – a children's doctor only she has some fancy name for it – but not on the National Health. And her husband's a civil servant, Income Tax, which you'd think'd make him unpopular too,' he added thoughtfully, 'but it doesn't seem to have done so far as I can tell.'

'That just leaves one couple, what did you call them, the Shelleys?'

'There's a big department store called Summerfields, not very far from Kenyon Court as a matter of fact, and quite near Earls-field Station. He's the manager of that. As for Mrs Shelley, she stays at home like a sensible woman.'

'Well, that's all very fine but it didn't take you very far did it?'

'Not so far as I'd have liked, guv'nor,' Jim admitted. 'I kept an eye on the place, on Sundays as I said, and I got to know the people who were regularly in and out, enough, I think, to distinguish the residents from the visitors, but a'course I didn't know which was which of the four families. Not until that Franklin walked in on me.'

'So I suppose now you're going to tell me you were looking for evidence as to who was responsible for the demands that were being made on you.'

Jim eyed him for a moment, obviously weighing up the advantages of frankness. 'Well, you see, guv'nor, it was like this,' he said at last. 'There was I wanting money, and not being able to raise it, though I'd'a' had plenty with what they'd took off me, and selling the shop besides. So it was only fair – wasn't it? – that the man who was responsible should come across with the cash. Something that was rightfully mine, as you might say.'

'Even though the contribution was made involuntarily,' said Antony. 'You're an ass, Jim, why didn't you come to me?'

'Oh well, Mr Maitland, I figured as how you'd done enough for me, you and Sir Nicholas. And there's another thing,' he added more hesitantly, 'I know you. Always poking your nose into things, danger or not. Would I want that on my conscience?'

'I didn't think you had one,' Antony told him frankly and earned another reproachful look.

'Is that a nice thing to say?' asked Jim in a hurt tone.

'I'll apologise if you like but I still say . . . oh well, it's done now and we have to make the best of it. What made you decide on Henry Franklin as the head of the protection racket? The retired owner of an antique shop sounds the least likely person.' He was picturing to himself as he spoke a tall thin stooped man with grey hair and long delicate fingers, a man quite unfitted for the difficulties of daily existence, certainly not the sort of person to cope with the likes of Stan and Alf. Unless of course . . .

'I did some thinking about all this,' said Jim, 'and it seemed to me the ground floor was the most likely place for Alf and Stan to be calling pretty well every evening. And being in the antique business he might have been a buyer,' Jim went on, completing his counsel's unspoken thought of a moment before, 'and that's how he got to know them. Besides, the other chap on the ground floor was away a lot, so it couldn't really be him.'

'Unless his wife was in it with him.'

'That's not a nice thing to suggest about a lady, Mr Maitland.' Jim was reproving again. 'So that left this chap Franklin, and if he was the one then he owed me something . . . see?'

'I suppose your decision to burgle his flat wasn't influenced in any way by the thought that the retired owner of an antique shop might have some valuable things about the place? As indeed turned out to be the case.'

'Fair's fair,' said Jim. 'You ought to know me better than to suggest a thing like that, really you ought.'

'It's because I do know you very well . . . however, perhaps we'd better forget all about that side of things. What made you think you could just walk in, with him and his wife in the bedroom, and help yourself to what you wanted and get away again?'

'I thought they was away.' It was Antony's distinct impression that Jim was more hurt by the implied slur on his professional ability than anything else. 'That's what Bill – my friend at the local shop – told me. Mrs Franklin had been in with a small order, "just some things for when we get back," she'd said, and added that they were going to visit her daughter in Barrow-in-Furness or some such place, who'd just had a baby. You can't blame me if they changed their mind.'

'Of course not,' said Antony seriously. 'So you thought the coast was clear. I expect you had a good look round.'

'Just in a couple of rooms. The coins caught my eye at once, because with things as they are now it was obvious they'd be all I needed.'

'It didn't occur to you that if Alf and Stan had in fact been making a delivery there'd be some cash around?'

'You're forgetting, guv'nor, I thought they was away.'

'So you did. Anyway, Jim, did you see anything to confirm your theory that Franklin was the man running the protection racket?'

'No, I can't say as I did. There wasn't a safe, I can tell you that, unless it was in the bedroom. I never got to see that.'

'I've no doubt you intended to.'

'I'd have been a fool not to, wouldn't I? She might not have taken all her jewels and such with her . . . but anyway, as I said I was content with what I got.'

'What made you look for a safe? I never heard –'

'And you're quite right, guv'nor, I never was a peterman . . . a safe-cracker,' he amended. 'When I was working regular, you know, if *that* was needed they'd send a bloke with me. But I was curious . . . wouldn't you have been? If he was what I thought he was he'd have needed a safe.'

'I see. And you only took the collection?'

'That's right. Those coins, even taken out of their cases, are heavy, you know. There were a few bits and pieces about, but I didn't think I'd bother with them.'

'And then you found that the Franklins weren't away after all. That was bad luck,' Antony sympathised insincerely. 'Well, you've given us something to go on, Jim, but there's one thing you haven't told us. Did you do any further research into Alf and Stan . . . who they really were for instance, and where they lived?'

'Not on your life They're dangerous men, Mr Maitland , and if they'd spotted me –'

'Yes, I see. However I'm sure after so many years you can describe them to us.'

'A couple of toughs,' said Jim readily.

'So you told us, but I don't think we could recognise them from that description, do you?'

'Now, Mr Maitland, you're getting ideas into your head.'

'Of course I am, Jim.'

'They're dangerous men.'

'And I should feel safer if I could recognise them before they had a chance of recognising me,' Maitland pointed out.

Jim looked doubtfully at Geoffrey Horton, and then back at his counsel again. 'All right then,' he said unwillingly. 'Stan is a squarish sort of chap, not very tall, in fact I wouldn't put him at more than five foot three. He has a round head and dark greasy hair rather long and straight and cut with a fringe. Looks weird, I can tell you.'

'What about Alf?'

'Oh, he's a different matter, built like a prize fighter but always

32

got up regardless. Fair hair, I wouldn't wonder if he had it waved,' said Jim disparagingly, 'but a good looking chap.'

'And formidable?'

'One of them would be bad enough, but two I wouldn't want to tangle with.'

'No, I see your point. What about their ages?'

'Thirty-five or a bit more, both of them, I should say.'

'Can you tell me any of the other shops in your neighbourhood who were being made to pay as you were?'

'I wasn't about to ask questions,' said Jim. 'Pay and keep your trap shut, that was my motto.'

'But somebody got beaten up, you said, and his store wrecked.'

'Yes, that's right enough, but all he ever gave out was that it was a robbery and he wouldn't recognise the chaps again. We all knew, of course, and we all knew it was no good asking any more questions.'

'What's his name, and what sort of a shop does he run?'

'Dan Tudor. He's a greengrocer with a florist's business on the side, but I think his wife looks after that. Walks with a limp now,' said Jim reflectively. 'To tell you the truth, guv'nor, I'm not too sorry to be in here at the moment.'

'All the same we'll have to see what we can do about getting you out, and safely on a plane to Toronto.' He was getting up as he spoke and Geoffrey followed suit, but Jim was staring at him incredulously.

'No chance of that now, guv'nor,' he pointed out. 'I mean it's one thing to hide what happened years ago, but something that's going on now –'

'I wouldn't be too sure of that.'

'And it was you who told me I shouldn't deceive the immigration authorities,' said Jim bitterly.

'I meant I shouldn't be so sure we couldn't get you on that plane. But don't get your hopes up, Jim,' he added, suddenly cautious. 'We may not be able to do anything.'

'I won't,' said Jim and Antony could tell he meant it. 'All the same I'm grateful to you, Mr Maitland, and you too, Mr Horton, for listening to all this rigmarole. But you won't let him get into trouble over it, will you?' he added to Geoffrey, in what he evidently thought was an aside inaudible to his counsel.

'I'll do my best,' Geoffrey promised. But he gave Antony an odd look when they got out into the street. 'I think you're mad,' he said.

'Why?' Maitland sounded only mildly interested.

'You're going to mix yourself up in this, I can tell it a mile off. And it's a dangerous business, Antony, best leave it alone.'

'And our client?'

'Put him in the box and let him tell his own story, you can elaborate on it in your closing speech. The one thing you can't do is get up in court and suggest that Henry Franklin is a – a gang boss,' said Horton despairingly.

'I know that, and I'll admit that what you suggest would be better than telling them he was drunk and didn't mean to steal anything. Besides, there's no proof at all that this Henry Franklin has been taking his money for years. We'd have to stick to how awful it was paying all this money for protection, how he was too frightened of Alf and Stan to put up the shop for sale, and how he was desperate to get to Canada. A lonely man, and growing old with his children three or four thousand miles away. Certainly this business of getting his own back would have to be left out.'

'I know that as well as you do.' Geoffrey sounded impatient. 'But you could make a good story of it.'

'I think at least we must identify Alf and Stan.'

'Cobbolds could do that for you.' And Geoffrey went on more urgently, when he saw that his friend still looked doubtful. 'It isn't as if we could get Jim his heart's desire no matter what we do. The immigration authorities aren't blind and deaf, and I don't suppose Canada is any more keen to take a crook on board than anyone else.'

'That's why I think we must prove who the principal really is. Then in addition to a good old sob story to tell the court we'd have the basis for some publicity that might soften the powers that be.'

All this time they had been making their way towards where their car was parked, but at this Geoffrey came to a full stop. 'I never thought I'd hear that from you, Antony,' he said. 'I thought you hated all journalists.'

'Hate is rather a strong word, though I must admit I can do with-out them most of the time. But don't you see, Geoffrey, if we can get this spread all over the papers I wouldn't mind betting they'd be sympathetic towards Jim's cause. Then if I can get Uncle Nick to pull a string or two –'

'If I know anything about Sir Nicholas,' said Geoffrey, again in his role of candid friend, 'by the time you finish with this business you won't be on speaking terms.'

'I don't think it will be as bad as that,' said Maitland thoughtfully. 'I think we must try anyway. And on consideration I think I'll find out about Stan and Alf myself.'

'If you mean to follow them about all over London . . . I don't know how long it is since you were in intelligence work, Antony.'

'A long time. And in another way not long enough,' he added, with unusual candour.

. 'Well then, best leave it to someone who's expert *now*.'

'If I make a mess of it,' Antony conceded. 'But they don't know me . . . remember?'

'I wouldn't mind betting they will before you're finished.'

'They never spotted Jim.'

'That's right, but –'

'They knew him,' Antony reminded him. 'Which means, I think, that they're pretty well sure of themselves, quite confident that their victims are sufficiently frightened of them to keep well away. So they made their journey from Fulham to Earlsfield looking neither to right nor to left, and always arrived conveniently during the dinner hour when it was unlikely that any other of the tenants would be about to see them. I wouldn't give tuppence for Jim's guess that Franklin was the man concerned though.'

'No, but none of the people in that building sound particularly likely. I wonder, Antony, can we trust his word about that? About these two men making for Kenyon Court every time, I mean.'

'That's one of the things I want to find out.'

They had reached the car now and he stopped while Geoffrey unlocked it and then got in and settled himself, much more at ease than he had been on the outward journey.

'And how do you propose to set about it?' asked Geoffrey, sliding into the driver's seat.

'Some time between now and next Monday I'll reconnoitre Don Tudor's shop, see if there's a good place where I can wait without drawing attention to myself. He's still on their list, you can be sure of that, and when they turn up I can take it from there. If they *do* end up at Kenyon Court eventually I can follow them in quite casually, they're not to know I'm not visiting one of the tenants.'

'But –'

'I shall try not to let them see me before they've rung one of the bells,' said Antony, forestalling his companion's objections.

'I don't like it, Antony. I suppose you're going to tell me that after that you'll follow them home.'

'Eventually, not that night I think. Seriously, Geoffrey, as long as they stick to public transport I'm home and dry.'

'It all sounds very specious. What am I supposed to be doing while all this is going on?'

'Preparing my brief. That shouldn't take you long, Geoffrey, the prosecution's case can hardly be complicated, and we only seem to have one witness, Jim himself.'

They were out in the traffic now, temporarily held up at a stop light. 'I should do that with more enthusiasm,' said Geoffrey, in rather a disgruntled tone, 'if I thought for a moment that you'd read the results of my labours.'

'Well, perhaps I shall have something to add to the pile of documents myself,' said Antony optimistically. 'No, seriously, Geoffrey, we have to do something for Jim.'

'Why?' asked Geoffrey curiously. 'I can see that nothing I say is going to stop you, but why? Is it because you feel a sense of obligation to Martha Arnold?'

'That's part of it I suppose.' If there was one thing that Antony hated it was the questioning of his own motives. 'And partly it's because Jim tried to deal with the situation himself without coming screaming for help to me. He must know he would have got it one way or another.'

'Yes, and I suppose he knows as well as I do in what way,' said Geoffrey grudgingly. 'You mean, I imagine, that he didn't want you to get hurt, and that's why he tackled the job himself.'

'Well, I think it was pretty decent of him on the whole,' said Antony. 'Bear with me, Geoffrey, I promise I'll be careful. And there's no earthly reason why Uncle Nick should know anything about it.'

'I thought you wanted him to use his influence.'

'I meant until it's all over.'

Geoffrey laughed suddenly, 'You're impossible,' he said. 'If I were a betting man, Antony, I'd give you whatever odds you care to name that Sir Nicholas will know exactly what you're up to before the end of the week.'

II

Geoffrey took him back to chambers, where they found Sir Nicholas about to leave for lunch. They all went out together, therefore, and no sooner were they settled at their favourite table at Astroff's than Sir Nicholas asked, 'How did your talk with Jim Arnold go? From what you've told me, Antony, there didn't sound to be much to be said in his favour.' The question was put in the most casual way possible, but both his hearers were perfectly well aware that Sir Nicholas very rarely spoke idly.

'Oh, he's given me a wonderful story, trust Jim for that. He says he was drunk, and didn't know what he was doing. Stealing was the last thing that was in his mind.'

'And I suppose the tools of his trade just happened to be in his pockets.'

'That's right, Uncle Nick.' He felt Geoffrey's eyes on him but went on airily. 'I don't think myself the jury will buy it, do you? But those are our instructions.'

At that moment, perhaps fortunately, the waiter came up and Sir Nicholas turned his attention to more serious matters.

Jenny's curiosity that evening was a little more insistent, and he was tempted to tell her the whole story for he had learned after many years that the one thing she couldn't stand was being kept in the dark. But she had tonight what he always thought of as her serene look, he couldn't quite bring himself to disturb her mood. Perhaps later if things got sticky . . . but there was no reason to think they would, he told himself. Except that the most ordinary matters have a way of doing so in your hands, his conscience reminded him, but he looked at Jenny again and did not listen.

So he told her just what he had told Sir Nicholas, and comforted himself with the reflection that it was after all the truth so far as it went. Jenny was a little saddened by Jim's fall from grace.

'He's been going straight so long,' she said. 'I'm sure they'll take that into consideration.'

'After I've pointed it out to them, of course,' said Antony, and wondered – for the hundredth time since that morning – whether Jim Arnold had really been telling him the truth.

FRIDAY, September 28th

Maitland had an idea in his mind that he hadn't disclosed to his instructing solicitor, and that was to get hold of Detective Chief Inspector Sykes of the Criminal Investigation Department at Scotland Yard and have an off-the-record chat with him. He had known Sykes for many years, and sometimes they had been allies and sometimes adversaries, but whichever way it turned out on this occasion he knew he could count on him as a friend. The relationship between the two men was a strange one, each feeling himself in some way under an obligation to the other and neither of them being the sort to take their obligations lightly.

He didn't have any luck the following day in running his quarry to earth, but on Friday morning he was lucky enough to find the detective momentarily at his desk. 'Well now, Mr Maitland, I hear you were trying to get hold of me yesterday,' said Sykes in his comfortable, north-country voice. 'And how is Mrs Maitland?'

'Well, very well. And so are my uncle and aunt,' said Maitland rather hurriedly, knowing well enough that this query would follow as the night the day immediately upon the other. Sykes was a man who liked to observe the proprieties.

'I'm glad to hear it. And yourself, Mr Maitland?' said the detec- tive, quite unperturbed. He was a man with his own dry sense of humour, which was not infrequently aroused in his dealings with Antony, and the familiar tinge of amusement sounded now in his voice.

'I'm very well,' said Antony impatiently. 'Could you spare me half an hour, Chief Inspector? Today if possible.'

'Yes, I thought it must be something urgent.' Sykes's voice conveyed somehow that he was settling himself down for a lengthy chat. 'I wonder what it could be now. I can't think of any- thing coming up this session that would be of interest to you.'

'Well, come and see me and you'll find out,' said Antony reason- ably. 'Not here,' he added, 'and I'd rather not come to you if you don't mind.'

'Some neutral ground,' said Sykes. 'It's a nice morning, Mr Maitland, if it is still a bit chilly. What do you say to a stroll in the park?'

'I think that would be a very good idea.'

'Or I've got a better one. I'll take the tube along to the Temple, and we can walk on the Embankment. That might save time for you if you're in a hurry, which is how you sound. I've nothing much on this morning.'

'That would be a help,' said Maitland with relief. 'Will you be leaving right away?'

'Right away,' Sykes affirmed. 'In case that happy state of affairs I mentioned to you a moment ago changes suddenly,' he added. 'Where shall we meet?'

'I'll be at the station,' said Antony, and rang off.

He was the first at the rendezvous, but Sykes wasn't very much behind him. In the event they didn't walk far, but came to a halt and stood looking down at the river, both of them quickly too absorbed in their conversation to notice the fairly stiff breeze that was blowing.

Sykes, having got his essential preliminaries over during their telephone conversation, came immediately to the point. 'What's to do then, lad?' he asked. Generally when he slipped into his native dialect it was when he himself was deeply moved, but in this case it was Maitland's only too obvious perturbation that prompted him.

A sort of reassurance, thought Antony wryly, I didn't know I'd got the jitters quite as badly as that. 'Do you think you could forget you're a police officer for a moment?' he asked abruptly.

'Well now, Mr Maitland, that might not be so easy. Suppose now I were to ask you to forget you're an officer of the court?'

'I couldn't do it, of course, it was a stupid question. What I'm try-ing to convey is that I want to consult you about something as a friend and not in your official capacity.'

'It seems to me we've had this conversation before,' said Sykes thoughtfully. 'You want to pick my brains, but you're not prepared to give anything in exchange.'

Antony laughed. 'Something like that,' he admitted.

'Well,' said Sykes carefully, 'I'll hear what you have to say, and I'll answer anything I think I can properly answer. But I can't promise to forget anything you tell me that can be regarded as police business.'

'Then I shall have to be careful what I say, shan't I? The thing is it involves the defence of a client of mine, and naturally I don't want the line we're taking to get back to the prosecution.'

'If it isn't one of my cases –'

'Nothing to do with murder,' Maitland assured him.

'In that case I think I can promise you discretion. But why should you think I can help you?'

'Because you always keep a finger on the grapevine,' said Antony mixing his metaphors in a way that would have offended his uncle. 'I've never known you yet when you weren't pretty fully informed, and not just about what's going on in your own department.'

'I take an intelligent interest,' Sykes agreed. 'Who is this client of yours anyway?'

'Jim Arnold.'

'Jim? Yes, I heard he'd been up to his old tricks again. But a very straightforward business from your point of view I should have thought.'

'Not quite so straightforward as it seems. I get the impression you're quite familiar with Jim's name, Chief Inspector.'

'Oh yes, we all knew Jim in the old days. And to tell you the truth,' said Sykes becoming confidential, 'I was very sorry to see him back in trouble again. Loneliness I expect you'll say, his wife dead –'

'But three years ago,' Antony reminded him.

'These things grow on you,' said Sykes. 'And there's those two kids of his, no more sense than to go off to Canada or Australia or somewhere like that and leave him alone. In the midst of temptation you might say. Not that I shouldn't have thought he was pretty well placed with that little shop and all. I understand there's no mortgage on it, so he must have done pretty well for himself, for his wife to be able to buy it outright while he was inside.'

'Yes, well, that's the sort of point I thought I'd be stressing when I first heard what had happened,' said Antony.

'And very well you'd have done it too,' said Sykes cordially.

'I don't know so much about that. It will still be a sob story,' he admitted, 'but not quite that one.'

'What then?'

'He says he's been paying protection money for about five years, that is since about two years after he took over the shop from his wife when he came out of prison. There's more to it than that, of course, but I think that's all I'd better tell you for the moment.'

'Do you know, Mr Maitland,' – Sykes was thoughtful again – 'that's the first time I've heard you admit to knowing more than you're willing to say.'

'Perhaps it is, but perhaps it's because on the previous occasions there's been nothing else. Anyway –'

'You want to know whether there's any chance that Jim's telling you the truth.'

'That's it exactly.'

'Well, Mr Maitland, as I said it's not precisely my line of country. All the same –'

'You do know something,' said Maitland accusingly.

'Summat and nowt,' said Sykes dampingly. 'If you're thinking I can put a name and a face to the person or persons responsible, I'm afraid you're in for a disappointment. And just because something has been going on – something always is, you know that, Mr Maitland – doesn't mean your client was one of the victims.'

Maitland ignored that for the moment. 'The shop is in the Fulham area,' he said.

'That's one of the districts involved.'

'Look here, Sykes, you seem to know too much and too little. If it's been going on for five years at least –'

'I'd say that was about the time the first reports came in.'

'What sort of reports?'

'Of the owners of small businesses being beaten up. The first time it happened it was thought to be a straight mugging, he had the day's takings on him and they'd gone, of course.'

'The chap concerned was on his way home?'

'That's right. Well he didn't say anything to contradict the theory, but a few things have happened since then that made it look a little different. The beatings would take place when the owners were alone in the shop, the place would be thoroughly wrecked, and whatever was in the till cleared out. But obviously it's easier to commit a robbery if you don't waste your time vandalising the place as well, so that made our people begin to wonder, you see. Only none of the victims would talk, and then again it began to be obvious it was because they were afraid. It got to Central when the DDI in Balham began to wonder if his was the only area concerned. Then a general enquiry went out and it became obvious that it wasn't just one district but about fifteen or sixteen that were involved, but of course we'd no idea at all how much the take was in each case or how many shops were involved. I shouldn't be telling you this you know, Mr Maitland.'

'It won't go any further.'

'So long as you don't think you can get up in court and use my evidence to prove that Jim Arnold is telling the truth.'

'I wouldn't dream of it. But if I could prove it from some other source —'

'Now there you have it, Mr Maitland, and that's why I think it's all a hum. Jim came to you with this particular story because he knew it was the kind of thing you'd fall for. I wouldn't mind betting he hadn't told his solicitor — was it Mr Horton again? — about it but insisted on talking to you in person.'

'Yes he did,' said Antony, rather taken aback. 'All the same —'

'You'd like to believe him, I know.'

'I don't see how, if all this has been under investigation for five years, you know so little about it,' Antony retorted.

'That's easy. I explained that at first there was no connection made between the different incidents, nobody would talk and it was quite a time before enquiries became really serious.'

'How did you set about it?'

'We had to start with the assumption that each district was worked separately on a different day of the month. The pattern of the incidents we knew about seemed to bear that out.'

'Wait a bit! How many incidents as you call them were there altogether?'

'You might have deduced that from what I told you, Mr Maitland, sixteen.' He paused a moment, and then added without

43

too much inflection in his voice, 'Two of the victims died.'

'So I was wrong when I said what I wanted to talk to you about had nothing to do with murder. But it wasn't very sensible,' said Antony. 'Killing the goose —' he added vaguely. 'So what did your colleagues do?'

'The obvious things. Asked questions at the shops nearby, where they were invariably met with perfectly straight faces and a categorical denial that anything was wrong. They also kept a watch on the shop of the injured man for as long as they could. That depended of course on the manpower in the local manor, as you know we're seriously understaffed. In one case I believe the surveillance went on for as long as six months, but nothing suspicious was observed, and as you can imagine it was a handicap having no description of the collectors.'

'You think it was the same man or men each time?'

'That would be guesswork, Mr Maitland, but there are two things in its favour. One's the M.O.' He expanded on that a little. 'The other . . . well, it's unlikely we know about all the districts involved, there may be some where no incident took place. But say there are twenty, and the men concerned — I'm speaking in the plural because I'm pretty sure there'd be at least two — keep a regular working week. That would keep them nicely occupied, wouldn't it?'

'I suppose you'll tell me next they're in a union of some sort,' Antony grumbled. 'And is that all you know about the affair?'

'Absolutely all, and as you see some of it is surmise.'

'What's the general opinion? Is it organised or haphazard?'

'Organised I'd say, and in a highly business-like way,' said Sykes promptly. Then his native caution took over. 'You must remember, Mr Maitland, I'm making an assumption, no more than that.'

'All this surveillance. Was nothing suspicious observed, didn't anybody — any couple if you prefer — turn up with suspicious regularity?'

'A lot of people did, but they all had good reasons for being where they were when asked.'

'What would that suggest to you?'

'That they'd leave the district well alone for a while after there'd been trouble. Organise a new one perhaps.'

'Or that they had reserves to call on.' He paused, realising that this didn't fit in altogether with Jim Arnold's story, but then neither did Sykes's suggestion. 'Tell me, Chief Inspector, what was the name of the man in Fulham who was beaten up?'

'I'm afraid I don't remember that.'

'But perhaps you remember whether Jim Arnold was questioned at that time. You said some of the small shopkeepers –'

'No, I'm quite sure of that. I believe in most cases the questioning was reserved for people whose shops were in the same street as the vandalised one. I think I'd have remembered if Jim's name had been mentioned in that connection.' He paused and gave his companion a rather quizzical look. 'Does all this help you at all, Mr Maitland?'

'Not a bit,' said Antony frankly.

'Which brings me to a question I've been wanting to ask you. What is your particular interest in Jim Arnold?'

'He's a very old client of mine,' said Maitland, vague again.

'I know all that. But I know you too, Mr Maitland, and the impression you're giving me at the moment is that you're about to embroil yourself up to your neck in what could be a very nasty business.'

'I –'

'It's no good, Mr Maitland, I know you,' said Sykes again. 'Take my advice, make the best you can of the story Jim's given you, and let it go at that. If you mix yourself up in the matter any further you won't be doing him a bit of good,' he added bluntly.

'I think I might. But to tell you why would involve me in those explanations I told you I don't want to give at the moment.'

'Well, you could at least tell me why Jim's future is so important to you.'

'I can't tell you that either. I don't think it can do any harm now, but it would be a long story, and it would involve breaking a promise I made to a woman who is now dead and therefore can't release me from it.'

'Always an answer for everything,' said Sykes, sighing. 'Well, you'll take your own way, Mr Maitland, no matter what I say, I suppose I should have known that to begin with. But don't forget what I told you. The kind of toughs who do the strong-arm stuff on these occasions are very unlikely to be organising such a complex operation. But they're at that man's disposal – if he exists and I think he does – and if you start one of your investigations you may very soon be out of your depth.'

'I'm grateful for the warning, of course,' said Antony, suddenly formal. 'But you'll forgive me, won't you, if I don't take your advice? And now let's get some lunch.' He straightened himself and looked about him as though he rather expected a restaurant might have sprung up in the vicinity while they were talking. 'Not Astroffs,' he said definitely. 'Can you suggest somewhere?'

From which simple remark Sykes divined correctly that Sir Nicholas Harding was not yet in his nephew's confidence.

Saturday luncheon with Sir Nicholas and Vera was another institu-
tion. Gibbs, quite impervious to his employer's wishes, would insist
on serving them himself or leave them to their own devices, as the
whim took him. That day he was in attendance throughout the
whole meal, and it was only when Vera said firmly, 'We'll have
coffee in the study,' that they were able to get a little time to themselves.

Afterwards Antony wondered whether Vera had sensed her
husband's frustration, it had been evident to him for a while that
there was some matter of which Sir Nicholas wished to unburden
himself. And, sure enough, as soon as they were settled and the
coffee poured he said in the gentle way that Antony over the years
had learned to distrust, 'I understand you've been trying to get in
touch with Chief Inspector Sykes.'

'He was a little elusive but I managed to get hold of him yesterday,' said Antony, knowing well enough that this apology for an
explanation wouldn't be the end of the matter. 'I suppose Mallory
told you,' he added. Old Mr Mallory was Sir Nicholas's clerk and
had been for many years, and though not quite so arbitrary in his
ways as Gibbs was sufficiently so to be something of a trial to the
younger members of chambers. 'It's coming to something,'
Maitland went on, 'if I have to go out to a public telephone box to
make a call.'

'My dear boy, if you make six calls in one day to the same
person, and then another three the following morning in fairly
quick succession, you must expect the fact to be noted. Are you
implying that there was anything secret about what you wanted to
say to Sykes?'

'Of course there wasn't.'

'Some personal matter perhaps?'

'No,' said Antony reluctantly. 'It had to do with a client's affairs.
We met and talked and he couldn't help me very much,' he added,

though he knew that it was but an idle hope to think that this would satisfy his uncle, who was obviously in one of his fact-finding moods.

'I see. One of your clients in whom you are taking a particular interest perhaps? And may I hazard a guess, Antony... Jim Arnold?'

'Well... yes.'

'We all had lunch together after Antony and Geoffrey had visited the prison,' said Sir Nicholas impartially to Jenny and Vera. 'Antony had some specious story about the defence he meant to put up.' His tone sharpened as he turned to face his nephew. 'I take it that was pure invention.'

'Nothing of the sort,' said Maitland indignantly. 'It was perfectly true that that was what Jim had told us.'

'But not, perhaps, the whole truth. You needn't think, my dear boy, that I missed the look Geoffrey gave you while we were talking.'

'Damn Geoffrey,' said Antony. 'Sorry, Vera,' he went on, without pausing to consider that the mildness of the expletive hardly warranted an apology.

'By all means, if you wish,' said Sir Nicholas cordially. 'However, I think – don't you, Antony? – that you owe me an explanation.'

'I'm not quite sure what you want me to explain, sir.'

'Then perhaps it would be simpler if I tell you my deductions,' said Sir Nicholas. 'No, Antony,' he added, stopping his nephew with a raised hand when he was about to speak, 'Jenny feels exactly as Vera and I do, we all like to know what's going on.'

'Yes, I know that's true,' said Antony, subsiding.

'But what is there to know?' Jenny demanded. 'It all sounded so simple, but now I don't understand at all. Of course, I know Antony feels a special obligation towards the Arnolds because of Mrs Arnold helping him once, but –'

'Yes I'm aware of that too,' Sir Nicholas interrupted her, 'but it's no excuse for his involving himself in some foolhardy escapade, to help a man who's brought all his trouble on himself.'

'It isn't quite as simple as that,' Antony protested. 'There *are* extenuating circumstances –'

'You told me, and you may get a jury to listen to you but

I doubt it.'

'There's more to it than that.'

'Just as I thought. Don't you think you'd better explain?'

'Yes, I suppose so.' He told them the whole story then, though rather more succinctly than he had heard it from Jim.

'Bad business,' said Vera when he had finished.

'I think the poor man deserves to get off,' said the ever tender-hearted Jenny.

'So where does all this take us?' asked Sir Nicholas.

'If I could prove the story is true —'

'About which you have some doubts yourself or I'm very much mistaken,' said his uncle.

'It would help if I could prove it,' Maitland repeated stubbornly. 'He might get away with a suspended sentence then, if the judge was in a good mood.'

'Which would still leave Jim Arnold in exactly the same position. And I don't know anything about the Canadian immigration laws —'

'Jim hadn't meant to tell them about his past,' Antony admitted.

'No, but something so recent . . . I don't think he'd have a chance of getting in.'

'That, you see,' said Antony rather hesitantly, 'is where I thought you might come in Uncle Nick.'

'Where *I* might come in?' asked his uncle, outraged.

'Yes, don't you see if we can get enough publicity about this affair, everyone would sympathise with Jim, and I thought *then* you could use your influence. The people on top, whoever they may be, could obviously bypass the rules if they want to. And I don't suppose they're any more hard-hearted than anyone else.'

'And you propose to obtain this publicity by exposing the man behind the — what shall I call it, my dear? — the racket?' said Sir Nicholas distastefully.

'Heard everything,' said Vera in her gruff way. 'Thought you hated the press, Antony.'

'Geoffrey said that, and I told him what I'm going to say to you: that hate is a strong word.'

'It isn't as if it was personal publicity he wanted,' said Jenny.

'Know that. Better go on, Antony, before Nicholas dies of

frustration. How do you propose setting about exposing this man?'

This was delicate ground but there was nothing for it but to explain the preliminary moves he had in mind just as he had done to Geoffrey.

'How much of this is due to your own desire to confirm Jim Arnold's story?' Sir Nicholas asked when he had finished.

'It will have that advantage,' Antony acknowledged. 'Or not, as the case may be. But the thing is, Uncle Nick, if you agree with me that the man behind the intimidation ought to be exposed I can't help feeling it would be a distinct advantage to put a scare into him, which we might do if we threaten to *subpoena* his minions. I'll take Geoffrey with me, of course, once I've identified them for myself,' he added hastily, before going on more slowly after a moment's reflection, 'If he'll come with me, that is.'

'You know perfectly well he'd follow you to hell and back if he thought it necessary,' said Sir Nicholas testily. 'As would any number of your other friends.' And it was a fact that Maitland was a man who was either very much liked (though often, as in Geoffrey's case, with a distinct note of exasperation entering into it) or very much disliked. With which latter emotion the look of amusement that all too often crept into his eyes very possibly had something to do.

'Nonsense, Uncle Nick, he's always reading me lectures,' said Antony, a little taken aback. 'Anyway, you do see what I mean, don't you?'

'It's an excellent scheme so long as you have no objection to getting yourself killed,' said Sir Nicholas cordially.

Jenny uttered an agitated squeak, and Vera, who was in her way more of a realist than her husband, said bluntly, 'Made up his mind, no use arguing.' Her speech, if anything, was more elliptical than usual today. 'Seems to me, Antony, *if* there's anything to find out, your proposal would be as good a way as any other. Two questions, though. Is there in fact such an organisation as you're postulating, and if there is, was Jim Arnold telling you the truth about what happened to him?'

'Which brings us,' Sir Nicholas pointed out, 'directly to what Chief Inspector Sykes had to say.'

'He thinks there's a well organised protection racket – I'm sorry,

50

Uncle Nick, I can't think of any other way of putting it – in existence, but I realise that doesn't prove anything.'

'At least you can tell us upon what he bases his opinion.'

'A lot of different districts are involved. The first case was a man who was robbed on his way home from the shop, that may have been just what it seemed, a mugging, or it may have been *pour encourager les autres,* like the later cases.'

'These other cases you speak of were different?'

'Yes. But I think the first one may have been undertaken on the collectors' own initiative. Afterwards they got instructions how to proceed. Anyway, since then, fifteen or sixteen men have been hurt, severely beaten in their own shops and their premises vandalised.'

'I don't know that I care for that word either,' said Sir Nicholas thoughtfully. And then, 'Perhaps you'll explain exactly what you mean by hurt, Antony.'

'That's all I know, all Sykes told me.'

'Except that –?' insisted his uncle.

'Except that two of them died of their injuries,' said Antony unwillingly.

'Very well then. What made the police connect these incidents together? Had they a description of the men concerned?'

'No description. The thing has been worked exhaustively, or so I gather, but no clues as to the identity of the men. They seem to have done a good job of scaring their victims' neighbours.'

'You didn't tell Sykes what you know?'

'No I didn't, not at this stage. He can keep his mouth shut, like the good chap he is, about the line of defence we're going to take, but he couldn't have ignored such an obvious invitation to police action.'

'I think you're right about that. What made him think, then, that the various incidents were connected?'

'The *modus operandi.* Except in the first case . . . that as I said was different and may not have been connected at all. Each man –' He broke off there, and glanced from Vera to Jenny, and changed the course of his sentence. 'The injuries were much the same in each case, and the systematic way in which the shops had been taken apart. But in thinking that one man ran the whole show I don't

51

think he had anything to go on but the fact that it's generally the case in these affairs. Anyway we know from Jim Arnold's activities –'

'So far unconfirmed,' Sir Nicholas reminded him. 'But tell me this, Antony, did anything Sykes told you tend to confirm Arnold's story?'

Antony thought about that. 'I wish I could say it did,' he said at last, 'but I can't. On the other hand –'

'Well?'

'Well, there's one discrepancy. I told you the police enquiries had been exhaustive, in one area where a man had been injured they kept surveillance in the immediate neighbourhood of his shop for six months. You can't tell me that two men going from shop to shop wouldn't have been noticed during that time.'

'How did you go about explaining that?'

'I wondered if they had sufficient reserves of – of collectors, as Sykes called them, to take care of the places where there had been trouble without being too obvious. There's an alternative to that, which he suggested . . . they might just have closed down operations in that area and gone on to a new one. There are endless possibilities. The trouble is, Jim Arnold says quite positively that he never saw more than two men, it was always the same two who called on him. And yet there had been an example made in Fulham, a greengrocer called Don Tudor.'

'Was Arnold questioned after that episode?'

'No, his shop – I don't think you ever saw it, Uncle Nick – was in a side street, nothing else near.'

'And the police's vigilance was not unnaturally concentrated in the vicinity of the unfortunate greengrocer,' said Sir Nicholas. 'If – what where their names, Stan and Alf? – had the sense to keep away from that quarter, they could still no doubt have done very well financially, without raising anyone's suspicion.'

'That's a point in Jim's favour, anyway.'

'On the contrary, Antony, it's nothing of the sort. I'm merely saying you've no proof either way. But if you're really determined –'

'Uncle Nick, I've got to do what I can.'

'Very well.' He smiled suddenly. 'On the strict understanding

52

that I've made no undertaking as to my own actions, even if you should prove your point up to the hilt.'

'We'll talk about that later,' Antony agreed. 'You were going to make a suggestion, Uncle Nick.'

'Yes, I think you should allow – what's the name of that firm of enquiry agents that Geoffrey uses?'

'Cobbolds.'

'That you should allow Cobbolds to do the first part of the enquiry. To tell you the truth, my dear boy, however expert you were at that kind of thing when you were involved with that gang of thugs in Whitehall, that's a long time ago and in any case you weren't acting completely single-handed. Cobbolds presumably have the men available to undertake this kind of thing.'

'Well, I –'

'I think it's a very good idea,' said Jenny enthusiastically. 'After all, Antony, you wouldn't want to do the poor men out of a job when it's right up their street, would you?'

Antony ventured a glance at his uncle and noted his pained look. 'You've got me over a barrel,' he said, deliberately adding fuel to the flames. 'But if you think –'

'Good idea,' said Vera. 'Don't turn it down just because Nicholas suggested it, Antony.'

'Am I likely to do that?' asked Antony blankly.

'Very likely, from what I've seen of you.' Vera softened this rather severe remark by giving him one of her grim smiles, which at one time would have scared the wits out of him but to which now he was quite accustomed.

'All right then, I'll do it that way since you're all ganging up on me,' Maitland agreed. 'There's one proviso though, I want to talk to this man Tudor myself . . . the greengrocer, in case you've forgotten. And also to Mrs Franklin, whom Geoffrey tells me isn't being called by the prosecution.'

'Franklin is the name of the man Jim Arnold robbed, isn't it?' asked Sir Nicholas.

'Yes, but it's such a clear case I don't suppose they think there's a need for any other evidence than his. Jim's never been one for violence, you know, and once he was discovered he waited quite peacefully for the police to come.'

'Think he'd have tried at least to make a run for it,' said Vera.

'Well, perhaps he might have done that, but the Franklins obviously have a telephone in their bedroom. The police arrived on the scene almost as soon as they did.'

'Well, those two visits seem ... not unreasonable,' said Sir Nicholas slowly. He glanced at Vera who gave him an abrupt nod, and then at Jenny whose eyes were on her husband's face. 'If you do as I suggest you should be safe enough,' he said, though Antony knew the addition, "if it weren't for your well known propensity for getting into trouble," was hovering on his uncle's lips, and only remained unuttered out of deference to the ladies.

'I'll phone Geoffrey this afternoon and tell him what we've decided,' he said, just to be on the safe side. But when his uncle spoke again it was obvious that his mind had gone off at a tangent.

'All I can say, Antony, is that I don't envy you when you get into court,' he remarked. But that wasn't all he had to say, not by any means, and by the time they went upstairs again about half an hour later both Antony and Jenny were heartily wishing that Sir Nicholas had a little less eloquence at his disposal, useful as he must find it in his profession.

PART TWO

Michaelmas Term, 1973

I

It was the following Friday when Maitland found time to begin his own investigations, and in the meantime he had cause to bless Sir Nicholas's suggestion that Cobbolds should be employed in the task of finding Alf and Stan. In other words, his professional duties kept him well occupied, and even Mr Mallory was inclined to be affable. Geoffrey Horton had punctiliously sent in a brief in the matter of the theft from Henry Franklin, giving at this point an edited version of Jim Arnold's story. That was safely in the pending file until something more was known, if that happy state of affairs were ever reached.

At first sight there was little sign that Don Tudor's shop had ever been the subject of vandalism, even some years ago, but Antony, who had learned young to be observant and never lost the trick of it, soon saw that repairs and painting had been done with an amateur hand. It was in two halves, the greengrocer's at the left, and a much smaller section on the right with cut flowers and house plants. There was something very attractive about the arrangement in that window. Jim Arnold had said – hadn't he? – that Don Tudor's wife was the florist. It would seem she had something of the artist in her.

However, in spite of the attraction of the flowers he made first for the greengrocery side. There was the usual pleasant smell associated with such places, but looking round him the thought occurred that one would soon get tired of living among turnips and potatoes.

There were two men in evidence, but one was no more than a boy, so Antony turned his attention to the other. 'Are you Mr Tudor?' he wondered.

'Yes, I am.' He was a pleasant looking man, but there was a certain wariness about his reply. Not very tall, and almost bald, so that the scar that ran from the top of his head to his right temple showed up angrily, and when he came forward it was with a decided limp.

'Is there somewhere we could talk alone?' Maitland asked him, and saw the other man's eyes narrow.

'You'd better come in back,' he invited.

Maitland followed him, aware that the boy's eyes turned on him curiously. 'You don't look like one of them,' said Don Tudor bluntly, turning to face him in the untidy little office at the back of the shop once the door was safely shut.

It was with difficulty that Antony resisted the temptation to take the short cut that was offered. 'I'm a lawyer,' he said. 'A barrister, to be precise. I'm representing Jim Arnold.'

'Are you now? I did hear Jim was in trouble.'

'I'm afraid he is and that's why I want your help.'

'There's nothing I can do as I can see.'

'Jim says there's a protection racket going on in this area, probably in others too.' He made a mental apology to his uncle as he spoke.

'Jim may have been paying protection, I know nothing about it. And Friday's a busy day, I ought to be helping the lad.'

'Mr Tudor, you were hurt weren't you? And your shop vandalised?'

'That was years ago, I've forgotten all about it. And nothing to do with what you're talking about.'

'Are you sure about that?'

'Quite sure.'

'How do you explain the episode then?'

'Robbery. They cleared the till, didn't they?'

'Yes, I'm sure they did. Are you telling me you resisted a straight hold-up? That was brave of you.'

'Soft-headed more like. That's how it was.'

'And it angered them so much that they injured you badly enough to send you to hospital? And then wrecked the shop?'

'I wasn't to know they was that sort. And I don't know that I like thinking back on it.'

'How much do you pay them, Mr Tudor?'

'I told you . . . nothing.'

'Yes, but you also said when I came in that I didn't look like one of *them*. What did you mean by that?'

'I've nothing more to say to you.' But he went on incautiously. 'How could I help Jim Arnold, anyway?'

'By backing up his story of what's been going on.'

'You'll not get me in court. And I don't see how it would help.'

'Extenuating circumstances,' said Antony vaguely. 'Believe me, Mr Tudor, I can understand your being afraid –'

'Not for myself I'm not.'

'I see. For your family then? I was going to ask you if I could talk to Mrs Tudor.'

'You leave her out of this.'

'Do they still make their collections in this district on the first Monday of the month?'

'You seem to know all about it,' said Don Tudor sulkily.

'Only what Jim told me. Well here's my proposition. If we know they're visiting you on Monday we could set a police trap for them.'

'You must be soft in the head. There'd be others.' It was a tacit admission and Maitland went on from there.

'You don't think, then, that the two men who visit you are the only ones involved?'

'Not on your life.'

'What makes you think that?'

'Things they've said.' He paused considering. 'We've no kids,' he said then, 'but there's the missus. You don't look like a man as would put a woman in danger.'

'If you tell me what you know it may help me. I'll give you my word not to have you called as a witness if you like. Not without your consent that is.'

'And you won't tell nobody?'

'My immediate colleagues, who are also men of discretion.'

Dan Tudor looked at him for a long time in silence. 'There's nothing much I can tell you,' he said at last, 'but I'm trusting you. The day they'd roughed me up, the day they'd wrecked the shop, I just said to them I wasn't paying any more. And one of them, the one they call Alf – I never heard their other names, said, "The boss won't like it, will he, Stan?" and the other one agreed. But I was daft enough to hold out and –' He broke off there staring at Antony. 'I'm trusting you,' he said again.

'I should have given you my name. It's Maitland. Antony Maitland.'

'That explains it then. Get yourself into the papers sometimes you do,' said Tudor, almost as if it was a matter for congratulation. 'But I never did hear as you let anyone down.'

'I won't, I promise. Have you anything else to tell me?'

'Only that I was still half conscious when they left. They said, "Don't forget, next time it will be the missus." That's why I've played ball ever since, and that's why I daren't –'

'No, I understand. How long were you in hospital?'

'Nearly a month.'

'And has Mrs Tudor been worried in the meantime?'

'No, that was a funny thing, they stayed away for a clear three months.'

'Did they ever give you any explanation for that?'

'Asked if I'd been lonely, ironic like. Said the rozzers had been around. Police,' he added, in case his hearer might not understand him. 'And made me pay three times the usual to make up.'

'What is the usual, Mr Tudor?'

'Now it's two hundred a month, it was less then of course. I don't remember exactly –'

'That's a lot of money. Can you afford it?'

'Well, the missus's side of the business – the flowers and stuff – brings in a bit. Means we haven't any savings though.'

'I'm sorry to hear that. But there are a number of shops on this street. Do you know positively that any of your neighbours are being intimidated in this way?'

'Not that I could swear to. Before . . . before my accident you know, I used to stand in the door and watch them go down the street from shop to shop. For all I know for sure they might have been buying something, and you'll not find anyone else that would be as open as I have.'

'I won't even try. That way it might get back to *them*' – he emphasised the word rather as Don Tudor had done – 'that someone was asking questions.'

'Well, that's good, but I don't see how I've helped you.'

You've convinced me of the truth of at least part of my client's story, thought Antony, but he didn't speak his thought aloud. 'Just take it from me that you have helped, Mr Tudor,' he said formally. 'I'm grateful for your trust and for the information you've given me. Can you add to your kindness by describing these two, it was always the same two men was it?'

'Always the same. The one called Stan was a little chap, quite a bit smaller than me, but very broad and strong-looking like a bull. Always looked a mess, black straight hair falling over his collar, don't think he washed it very often. Alf, now he was a real bruiser, but always beautifully turned out. Quite a dandy.'

'I see. Now do you think —' But before he could formulate his request the door burst open and a little bustling woman with a round pleasant face that made her look very like her husband came in. She didn't speak immediately but closed the door carefully behind her and leaned against it. 'Mickey's busy,' she said. 'Everything all right, Don?'

'Quite all right, Mavis. She doesn't know anything,' he added to Maitland.

'Anything about what?' she asked suspiciously.

'We were talking about how your husband got hurt,' said Antony. 'You weren't here that day?'

'What's that to do with you?'

'He's a lawyer,' said Don pacifically. 'The one we've read about sometimes. Mr Antony Maitland.'

'That's all very well, but what does he want with us?'

'You needn't worry, Mrs Tudor. Your husband has helped to — to settle my mind on one or two points, but I assure you the matter will go no further. Did you know what was happening when the requests for money first started?'

She glanced doubtfully at Don Tudor, but for some reason that Antony couldn't fathom the exchange of glances seemed to reassure her. 'Nothing at all,' she said. 'I did wonder sometimes why we were always short of cash, but Don did the books and just told me the expenses were getting very much heavier. Which was true in its way. He never let me come in on Mondays. Well it was reasonable really, no trade that day in my line, so when he suggested I took time off to see to things at home I agreed. But when he was hurt, when he was in hospital I made him tell me.'

61

was hurt, when he was in hospital I made him tell me.'

'What is your usual routine? Does your assistant – Mickey did you call him? – know anything about it?'

'I didn't have an assistant before it happened – the accident I mean,' said Don, who seemed to prefer this way of putting it. 'Only I'm not so quick on my pins now. First time they came I brought them in here and they talked to me pretty straight, and for a while I handed over the cash rather than make any trouble. When they started coming again after Mickey was helping me I used to bring the money in here and have it ready for them. That prevented any questions.'

'Have you seen the two men since that time, Mrs Tudor?'

'Made it my business to. Brutes,' she said.

'Have you been in here when the money was handed over?'

'No, Don wouldn't let me. But I'd stand in the arch between the two shops, and watch them going out. Pretty regular in their times they always are.'

'Your husband thinks if we set a police trap for them it will be known he's been talking, and someone else would take over and exact a revenge.'

'Yes, I think that too,' she said hurriedly. 'I don't want Don to get hurt again.'

'Your husband thinks they weren't in it alone.'

'Those two? No.'

'I wonder if you ever heard anything that would confirm that, or perhaps help me to identify their principal.'

'Not really,' she said doubtfully. 'One day as they were walking back through the shop – it was the day they put their price up, Don told me later – one of them said to the other, Stan I think it was, "Nice little haul." And then he added, "I wonder what an old geezer like that does with it all".'

'But that might be very helpful. Thank you, Mrs Tudor.'

'Really?' Her eyes were searching his face as though she doubt-ed the truth of his statement, but she sounded gratified all the same. 'Are you trying to stop it?' she asked.

'I'm trying to help Jim Arnold, who was the source of my infor-mation in the first place. But if we put a stop to the racket while doing so that would be all to the good. I may speak to you again,

Mr Tudor, when I know more about this question of a police trap. I still think it could be done without involving you in any way.'

'If you think so,' said Don doubtfully.

'If it can be it should be,' said Mrs Tudor more robustly, but her husband followed Maitland to the door of the shop.

'Remember what I told you they said to me about Mavis,' he remarked by way of valediction. 'She doesn't know they threatened her, but I can't forget it.'

'And I won't either,' Maitland assured him. 'I'm very grateful to you, Mr Tudor, and that's something else I shan't forget.'

II

Maitland went back to the Temple and then out to lunch with his uncle. He had hoped to avoid altogether a controversial subject, but naturally Sir Nicholas demanded an account of his morning's activities. 'So you see, Uncle Nick,' Antony concluded, 'Jim was telling the truth about the financial demands on him, and about the two men called Stan and Alf as well.'

'Yes, I see that. However,' Sir Nicholas pointed out, 'you still have no confirmation of the fact that he ever followed them to Earlsfield.'

'No,' Maitland admitted. 'Still, you must admit it's a beginning.'

'If all you want is to convince yourself —'

'No, of course, that's the least of my troubles.'

'Mallory tells me that Geoffrey Horton rang you this morning. He left a message to say that he had Cobbold's report now.'

Maitland glanced at his watch. 'I made an appointment with Mrs Franklin, and I think I'd better go straight from here,' he said. No good annoying the lady by being late. 'So would you mind asking Willett to phone Geoffrey and get him to bring the report to chambers about half past four, if that's convenient for him. I should manage to be back by then.'

'If you're later you'll find him in my room,' said Sir Nicholas. 'If I'm to become responsible for Jim Arnold's future, I have at least the right to know the truth about this story of his.'

'Yes, of course, Uncle Nick.' This was still a delicate subject and Antony's tone was conciliatory. For the rest of the meal he managed to steer the conversation in another direction, and left as soon as he had finished, leaving Sir Nicholas sitting over his coffee.

The way to Kenyon Court was not quite so simple, starting from the City, as the route Stan and Alf were alleged to have taken from Parsons Green. However, the underground seemed the best means of transport for his purpose, and after leaving the station at Wimbledon Park he found his way to the block of flats with only a couple of false starts. The first person of whom he enquired was a stranger to the district, the second gave him explicit directions which turned out to take him right out of his way, but the third was a local man and wrote his recommendations on the tattered envelope that Antony produced from his pocket. When he rang the bell of Flat Number Two he was only five minutes later than he had said.

Rita Franklin opened the door to him. She was a tall woman with dark hair, rather rigidly waved, and at the moment a look of amusement which Maitland found inexplicable. 'Come in, Mr Maitland,' she invited. 'I can't think how I can possibly help you, but I did as you asked and sent Henry for a walk.'

'I hope he didn't mind,' said Antony, following her as she backed away from the door. 'It would be contrary to custom for me to have any conversation with him about the case, but a mere glimpse of each other wouldn't have done any harm.'

'Well, I thought it was best to be on the safe side.' The room to which she took him was large and square, a modern setting for some very old things. But Antony, as he looked round, was mentally congratulating Henry Franklin on his taste. He had managed to combine a liking for the antique with a fair degree of comfort, which in Maitland's experience wasn't often done. 'You'll find that chair over there by the fireplace quite comfortable, Mr Maitland,' said Rita Franklin still with that note of amusement in her voice. She seated herself composedly, folded her hands in her lap and waited.

The chair was indeed very comfortable. 'You understand the position, Mrs Franklin,' Antony said. 'I'm representing James Arnold, the man you caught burgling the flat. I can't talk to your

64

husband, I gather you realise that, but you're not being called by the prosecution so I should like to hear what you can tell me about that night.'

'It seems a bit odd to base your defence on what one of the injured parties has to say,' she told him. 'And when I say "injured party", I couldn't care less about those old coins really, but naturally I'd rather Henry was happy than not. And to have lost them would have been a real tragedy for him.'

'One swallow doesn't make a summer,' said Antony rather vaguely, but added, seeing her look of incomprehension, 'I meant of course, one witness doesn't make a case.'

'No, I see. Still it seems odd,' she insisted. 'However, I'm sure you know your own business best. What do you want me to tell you?'

'Your husband's retired, isn't he?'

'Yes, he's sixty-two you know' – a good deal older than you are then, was Maitland's mental comment – 'and when he was sixty he just said he'd had enough. It was getting more and more difficult to find assistance, he couldn't spend his whole time at the shop, and quite frankly the general public were beginning to get on his nerves.'

'That doesn't surprise me,' said Maitland rather dryly. 'I hope you're both enjoying his retirement.'

'Oh yes, when we were both working we saw little enough of each other. So when he sold the shop I decided to leave my job too.'

'I didn't know –'

'How should you? I was a journalist. Do you read the Courier?'

'Most days. My father used to work for them a long time ago.'

'Did he though? Could that be where I've heard your name before?'

'I don't think so, it must have been long before your time.' He didn't amplify that or add that, his father's profession notwithstanding, he hadn't much time for journalists himself nowadays. Some of his own more unorthodox proceedings had been the subject of not altogether charitable comment in the press. 'I'm afraid I don't often notice bylines though,' he added.

'Oh, I wasn't on the reporting staff, and I don't suppose you trouble with the women's pages. I still do a little work for them, an odd article here and there as the spirit moves me. I'm not a particularly domesticated person, so it gives me an illusion of still doing some useful work.'

'You have a very beautiful room.'

'Yes.' This time she smiled at him quite openly. 'There were a few fights about that, I can tell you, Henry would sacrifice comfort to what he regards as beauty any day. I don't think the compromise worked too badly do you?'

'I think it worked very well indeed. Your husband owns Kenyon Court, doesn't he?'

'Yes, it seemed a good investment to make when we both retired, or rather, in anticipation of our retirement, though I admit that again was my influence. Henry would have chosen an old place, probably falling to pieces and let us in for endless repair bills.'

'This seems a nice area.' Antony was speaking as casually as he could. 'I hope your tenants don't give you too much trouble. If Mr Franklin was tired of the general public –'

She laughed again. 'We consider ourselves very lucky,' she said. 'I don't think it's likely you'd find three couples anywhere in a place like this who are completely congenial, or whom we wanted to make close friends of. But they don't cause any trouble and they do pay their rent on time.'

'And that after all is the main thing,' Maitland agreed. 'Your neighbours on this floor for instance –?'

To his relief she fell willingly enough for the lure of silence. 'The Priors?' she said. 'Archie is a civil engineer, and naturally that takes him away a great deal. When he's home we usually make a point of getting them round to dinner, and I must say I like him very much. Joyce we know a good deal better because she used to be Henry's assistant. It wasn't her I was talking about when I spoke of the difficulty of getting help, I ought to explain that. It's the – the underlings. Anyway, Joyce is very capable, and now she runs the place for the new owner.'

'How old a couple are they?'

'Archie is about Henry's age, but I don't think he has the faintest idea of retiring until he's driven out. Joyce – well I must admit I've never known exactly how old she is, probably about fifty or fifty-five, but I'm judging by the things she says rather than how she looks. She's full of energy, and very attractive really. In fact I used to tease Henry about her when they were working together all the time, but it was just for fun, I never had the slightest doubt about him.'

'If Mr Prior is so often away, I dare say it's Mrs Prior who looks after their business affairs,' said Maitland, taking refuge in vagueness again.

'Oh yes, and I think she probably would anyway He strikes me as a little vague about that sort of thing though I'm sure he knows his own profession through and through.'

'So it's she you have to thank for the regular rental payments,' said Antony, smiling.

'That's right.' She gave him a straight look. 'For some reason you're interested in the other people living here, Mr Maitland.'

'Yes, I am as a matter of fact,' said Antony. 'Not exactly as persons, but in how easy, or otherwise, they are to get on with and how well they meet their obligations. You see,' he went on, improvising hastily, 'my wife and I have our own quarters, our own flat as you might say, at the top of my uncle's house. But it's by no means self-contained, and since he married a couple of years ago —' He let the sentence trail there, hoping it sounded effective, and this time making his mental apology to Vera.

'Your uncle is Sir Nicholas Harding, isn't he? I must admit that it was partly curiosity that made me say I'd see you today. I may not actually be on the reporting staff but I know most of them, of course, and I've heard your name mentioned many times.' She gave him a shrewd look. 'You don't like me to say that, Mr Maitland.'

'Not much,' he admitted. 'But to get back to what I was saying, Jenny and I have often talked about what we might do if we leave the house in Kempenfeldt Square, and there's no doubt a place like this, not too large, but with a little something coming in —' He broke off again, and again she came to his rescue.

'It's ideal in many ways,' she assured him, 'but I've already told you we're lucky enough in our tenants, the way they all pay their rent on time.'

'Jenny's home all day. I wouldn't want her to have to put up with a lot of people coming complaining.'

'Well, the first thing of course,' she assured him seriously, 'is to see that there's nothing to complain about. Then vet them pretty well before you sign the lease.'

'Is that what you did?'

'Not exactly. The Dickinsons and the Shelleys were here already when we bought, and Joyce, naturally, we knew well.'

'I see.'

'Still, it's good advice. I don't think there's any way of being absolutely sure, but at least if you're careful you shouldn't do too badly.'

'That's very reassuring. You get on just as well with the people upstairs, then, as you do with the Priors?'

'Oh yes.' He was pretty sure his story didn't deceive her for an instant, which was a pity, but couldn't be helped. At least it had had the desired effect of making her talk. 'The Dickinsons live above us, Rufus and Mamie. And since I've been so frank with you Mr Maitland, I must admit she's the nearest thing to being a difficulty here.'

'How is that?'

'She's an American, which – if they hadn't been here already – would have probably led me to urge Henry to let them have the place. I did two or three tours in New York in my younger days, for the newspaper, the dress shows, and shopping on Fifth Avenue, and the rag trade in general, and everyone was always so kind to me I must admit I've rather a soft spot for them. But Mamie can be ... just a little scratchy. She's a doctor, a paediatrician she calls herself, with a private practice because she won't have anything to do with socialised medicine; she says the American Medical Association would never stand for it. And then she's a very fervent Woman's Libber, and that doesn't go down awfully well with the rest of us.'

'How does it go down with her husband?' asked Antony, smiling.

'I think he's very patient with her, but Henry's not quite so charitable. He says Rufus is too unimaginative to take any notice when she says outrageous things. He's a civil servant, fairly high up in the Inland Revenue Department I believe, and he hasn't very much sense of humour, but enough to assure you that you mustn't hold his occupation against him. But I still say I'm right about them . . . he's patient with her because he's very much in love with her.'

'I suppose,' said Maitland reflectively, 'that two congenial couples out of three, or should I say five congenial people out of six, isn't bad going.'

'You mean the Shelleys, they're both dears. He manages one of the big department stores, Summerfields, your wife would know about it if you don't.'

'And what does Mrs Shelley do?'

'Alfreda? She's what's usually referred to nowadays as "just a housewife". I think she enjoys that role very much. In any case she'd be retired by now as I am, they're both over sixty.'

'It sounds encouraging,' said Maitland. 'Though perhaps, as Jenny's home all day, it would be better to look for tenants who were both working.'

'As for that, I like to have Alfreda around. We get together sometimes for coffee in the morning or tea in the afternoon, Henry still likes to attend some of the auctions, and I'm not particularly good at being alone.' She had been answering his questions willingly enough, but Antony wasn't altogether surprised at the cynical look she gave him at this point. 'For some reason you're interested in all of us here at Kenyon Court,' she said, and held up her hand as he was about to speak. 'No, don't tell me again, I don't believe for a moment you've got a personal reason for all this. Are you going to explain it to me?'

'There's only one answer to that. No,' said Antony baldly.

To his relief she laughed. 'Well, that's frank at any rate. I think you said at the beginning that you were interested in knowing exactly what happened that night. Was that a – a terminological inexactitude as well?'

'No, it was perfectly true. Mrs Franklin –' he added impulsively.

'Yes?'

'I was only going to apologise for being rather mysterious, but I'm sure you'll understand that I can't talk about my client's affairs.'

'Yes, of course I understand, and it may seem odd but I think I'd help you if I could. Only there's nothing to tell about that night.

We heard a noise, it must have been about two in the morning but I didn't notice that at the time. Henry thought immediately of his collection of coins, and rushed out to protect them without even putting his slippers on. By the time I'd followed, decently covered, he'd picked up the poker and was confronting this man whom I suppose is your client. Not a very impressive looking man, but I imagine under the right circumstances rather likeable. He certainly wasn't violent, he waited quite patiently until the police came, which wasn't very long as I'd already called them from the bedroom. Of course he might have thought Henry was prepared to use the poker. And when the police arrived, his pockets were stuffed with the coins. Henry had already discovered that the case was empty, of course, but I stopped him from making – what's his name, James Arnold? – I stopped Henry from making him turn out his pockets.'

'From the prosecution's point of view that was wise of you. There's just one other thing, Mrs Franklin.'

'Yes?'

'I believe there was some talk of your going away.'

'Yes, we were going to see my daughter who lives in the North and has just had a baby. Our first grandchild. But then Henry started with a cold, and of course we didn't want to take any infection with os, so we decided to put off the visit. Until this month, as a matter of fact, only now it may be difficult. I'm not sure when the case will come on.'

'Neither am I yet.'

'Well, whenever it is Henry will have to be there.' She smiled again. 'You weren't thinking of calling me, Mr Maitland?'

'No, I've no idea of doing that.'

'All the same I think I shall be in court, it sounds as if you might have something interesting up your sleeve. What can you do though, in a clear case like this? My writing was always from a woman's angle, I never understood much about the law.'

'There are always a number of options open to one,' said Maitland rather vaguely. 'The trouble is choosing the right one. But in this case' – he returned her smile – 'I think I shall have to say wait and see.'

'Yes, I suppose you must.'

'Which reminds me, though I don't know why it should, of one more question. Is the main door here, the door that's common to all the flats, left open all night?'

'No. Henry generally puts the latch down at about eleven. All the tenants have keys, of course, but if any of us has visitors they don't need a key to get out.'

'Thank you. That really is all.'

'Would you like some tea before you go, Mr Maitland?'

'No, I've got to get back to chambers for a conference. Besides I dare say Mr Franklin will be back at any moment, and it would be just as well if we don't meet.'

'Well, I must say it's all very silly,' said Rita Franklin. 'But I suppose you know your own business best.' She came to the door with him and said seriously as he turned to thank her again for her help, 'Perhaps you should think of investing in this kind of place after all. Something just like this would be ideal, people don't go in for the old-fashioned as much as they used to now. They like all mod. cont. as the advertisements say.'

'Perhaps we should,' he agreed. 'But I'll tell you something, Mrs Franklin, since you've been so kind and not taken offence at my questions, Jenny and I are really very comfortable where we are.'

III

As he had anticipated he was a little late for his appointment with Geoffrey, but Sir Nicholas had kidnapped the solicitor firmly and taken him into his own room, and they were both poring over a lengthy-looking document when Maitland arrived.

'Is that Cobbold's report?' he asked, without waiting to exchange greetings.

'It is,' said Geoffrey, 'and a very comprehensive one too.'

'Well, out with it. Is Jim Arnold telling the truth or not?'

'I thought you'd already convinced yourself of that,' said Geoffrey, with a tinge of sarcasm in his tone.

'As I told Uncle Nick at lunchtime, his story was true insofar as the fact that the protection racket actually exists. But I don't know about the rest of it. About following Stan and Alf, about the reason he went to Kenyon Court.' He turned to his uncle for a moment.

71

'I've been talking to Mrs Franklin,' he said. 'She's a nice woman, I hope Jim isn't right about her husband being the one involved.'

'You're thinking that if he was she must be too,' said Sir Nicholas.

'Something like that. It's difficult to see how a couple in a place like that could have had any secrets from each other.'

'Now you're theorising ahead of your data,' said his uncle reprovingly. 'When you've read this report –'

'When Geoffrey has given me the gist of it,' said Maitland firmly. He turned to his friend. 'Do I gather it's not quite what we expected?'

'Yes and no,' said Geoffrey annoyingly. 'I told Cobbolds to start out by assuming that what Jim told us was true, if it was that would make their task of shadowing the two men a good deal easier. They picked them up in Fulham, and it was exactly as he said.'

'I knew it!'

'A moment ago you professed to be in some doubt,' said Sir Nicholas dryly.

'Well, all right then, Uncle Nick, I hoped he was telling the truth. There's more than that, isn't there, Geoffrey?' he added, looking more closely at the solicitor.

'A good deal more. Jim's description was a pretty good one, as you remember, and it wasn't very difficult for the man at the Kenyon Court end to recognise two types arriving at the time Jim Arnold mentioned, and not looking at all like tenants. So he wandered across and walked in quite openly as if he were visiting somebody living there. If they were on their way upstairs he intended to knock at one of the ground floor flats, ask for some fictitious name, and make his apologies for a mistake. On the other hand if it was one of the ground floor flats that was their destination it would have been much easier, he could have walked upstairs and probably on the way seen exactly who was involved.'

'Something went wrong with that idea?'

'Let's say it didn't work out as he expected. The bigger of the two – that's Alf, isn't it? – was carrying a briefcase and when Cobbolds' man went in he had just unlocked a door under the staircase and put it down inside, taking another one out as he did so. Cobbolds' man went straight upstairs as he had planned to do

72

in other circumstances, and had a good look at the cupboard when he came down. There was a Yale lock on it, nothing very compli cated, but it was enough to deter anyone respectable from looking inside. So you see –'

'I see that adds to the probability that Henry Franklin is the man we're looking for. He of all people could make that arrangement.'

'And without your friend Mrs Franklin knowing,' Sir Nicholas put in.

'Yes, quite so. All the same it's possible –'

'What's possible?' demanded his uncle after the silence had lengthened for a moment.

'Well, from what I've seen of modern flats they're sometimes pretty short of storage space. Supposing one of the other tenants has some belongings they didn't want to dispose of, but couldn't keep in the flat conveniently. Franklin, as the owner, might have arranged for any one of them to have the use of that locked cupboard.'

'That's true. Could Mrs Franklin tell us, do you suppose?'

'I don't know if that would be altogether a wise move,' said Geoffrey. 'We don't want to alert the guilty party, and even if neither she nor her husband is involved such a query might easily get back to their neighbours.'

'Especially as she seems to be on good terms with all of them,' said Antony. 'Yes, I agree that wouldn't be a good idea, but not because I don't want the guilty party alarmed . . . I do. But not just yet. Perhaps you think I shouldn't have called on Mrs Franklin either, Geoffrey.'

'I can't see that it could do any harm, or I'd have protested about it. I can't see what good it did though.'

'Not much, except that I got a sort of description of each of the tenants, enough to know that any of the men might fit the descrip tion Alf and Stan applied to their principal when they called him an old geezer. Which only puts them in their early sixties, Uncle Nick,' he added apologetically, 'but you know how loosely people talk.'

Sir Nicholas smiled at him in a way that rivalled Vera's for grim ness. 'As I expected you to obtain no material information I suppose I must congratulate you on your success, my dear boy.'

'Yes . . . well . . . what came next, Geoffrey?'

'They can't go any further than watching the house, because of course anyone lurking inside would be spotted immediately, so I don't see what more Cobbolds can do about the receiver. But I haven't quite finished, Antony.'

'No, of course, you're about to wave your wand and lo and behold Alf and Stan will no longer be lay figures, but creatures of flesh and blood.'

'If you care to put it that way,' said Geoffrey a little stiffly. 'This bit was more difficult, which is why the report has been so long coming in. The details are all there.' He waved his hand towards the document he and Sir Nicholas had been studying.

'I don't want the details,' said Antony. 'Just the outcome.'

'Very well then,' said Geoffrey in a resigned tone. He had known Maitland long enough to be aware when it was useless to argue. 'Alf is Alf Gray, and Stan is Stan Bond, and they both live in Balham.'

'Records?' said Antony sharply.

'Oh yes, they've both been inside too. Robbery, and robbery with violence, but the impression is that they're both a bit dim and neither of them has ever been involved in doing his own planning. The chap they used to work for is doing ten years.'

'I wonder how they got this assignment. It must have seemed like a piece of cake to them.'

'I dare say it did,' said Geoffrey, with a sidelong apologetic glance at Sir Nicholas's pained expression. 'Anyway, their addresses are there if you can be bothered to turn the pages. The question is, where do we go now?'

'Eventually to the police,' said Antony promptly. 'But before we do that I think we should see Alf and Stan, perhaps we can even scare them into giving us their present employer's name.'

'That is obviously a matter that can best be handled by the police,' said Sir Nicholas coldly.

'But, Uncle Nick, you've always hated it when I get involved with them.'

'Laying information can hardly be called being involved,' said his uncle, still icily.

'But no harm could come of talking to the two men first,' said

Antony, more persuasively now.

'How do you know that?'

'Because I shall have Geoffrey with me, and I'll bet he can scare them more effectively with talk of *subpoenas* than a bodyguard of a hundred policemen could.'

Sir Nicholas looked at him for a long moment. 'Very well then,' he said at last. 'I see you're quite determined. When do you propose that these interviews should take place?'

'Early tomorrow morning is the obvious time, I should say. If that's all right with you Geoffrey,' he added.

'As all right as any other time,' said Geoffrey rather disagreeably.

'Catch them before they're quite awake,' said Antony. 'What's the betting they go on a binge on Friday night after they finish work? We'll try Alf first,' he added thoughtfully, 'since he's the larger of the two.' And turned to meet his uncle's look of outrage with one of the blandest innocence.

SATURDAY, October 6th

I

Alf Gray, on enquiry at the address Cobbolds had given them, proved to be unmarried, and to live in a single room 'with facilities' in a house that was surprisingly well kept considering the way the neighbourhood had gone down in recent years. The landlady herself, however, was a rather slatternly woman, who was in some doubt about the propriety of rousing her lodger at so early an hour. 'I'm sure you'll find that's all right, Mrs Er,' said Geoffrey, at his best in situations like these. 'He wouldn't want to miss what we have to tell him.' He had called for Antony early enough that morning to have breakfast with him and Jenny; Maitland's injured shoulder made it uncomfortable for him to drive himself, and though various kind friends had pointed out to him from time to time that it was possible to get a car with special controls he's always resisted the idea, and even now continued to do so no less vehemently.

'All right then,' said the woman doubtfully. 'He's in the first floor front, but don't say I didn't warn you. And don't let him blame it on me.'

'We wouldn't dream of doing so, madam,' said Geoffrey, and led the way towards the staircase. A moment later he was rapping urgently on what proved to be the right door.

Alf took some rousing. At length there came a kind of moan from within, and the creaking of bed springs; and finally the sound of some heavy weight deposited on the floor. Even then it was a few moments before footsteps crossed the room and the door was flung open.

Just as he had been described, Alf was an enormous man, who might well have been familiar in the prize ring, or in a wrestling contest. Just at the moment he was in no condition to show his normal dapper appearance, as he was wearing rumpled pyjamas,

76

his hair was untidy, and he had a day's growth of stubble. He looked at the pair on the threshold in a lowering way. 'Is that the way to go on?' he demanded. 'Rousing a chap from sleep when he's having a lie-in.'

'We must apologise to you, Mr Gray,' said Geoffrey, moving forward remorselessly as he spoke. 'I'm afraid our business with you is urgent.'

'Who are you then?' asked Alf backing away a little, sufficiently so at least as to allow Antony to join his friend and close the door behind them. A quick glance round informed Maitland that there was no telephone in the room. Less chance then that when they had dealt with this member of the partnership he would have time to warn his colleague of their impending arrival.

'Lawyers,' said Geoffrey succinctly.

'What do you want with me?' His hackles went up immediately. 'I'm not in any trouble.'

'Don't you think so, Mr Gray?' put in Antony from Geoffrey's shoulder.

'I should know, shouldn't I?'

'You should indeed. Didn't it occur to you when Jim Arnold was arrested that there might be . . . repercussions?'

'I don't know what you mean.'

'That his arrest, and what he might say to his lawyers, might have some effect on you,' Antony explained. Geoffrey, who knew well enough when his friend had the bit between his teeth, was quite content to stand back and give him his head. 'We're his lawyers you see and I think I may say old friends of his. Mr Horton here is his solicitor, and I'm his counsel.'

'What's that got to do with me?'

'Mr Horton is preparing Jim's defence. Perhaps he can answer that question better than I can.'

Geoffrey took the cue. 'There's some idea, Mr Gray, of calling you and your friend, Mr Bond, as witnesses.'

'You wouldn't dare.'

'On the contrary, in our client's interest —'

'There's nothing we could tell as'd help him.'

'Oh, but I think there is.' That was Maitland again. 'You could explain to the court all about the protection racket, and how you

77

hounded Jim into crime by your increasing demands.'

'Here!' said Alf. He'd backed away a good distance by now and was scrambling into the trousers which had been laid along the foot of the bed. If he had been bleary-eyed when they first entered the room he was rapidly regaining his composure now. 'If Jim's been making up stories it's nothing to do with me.'

'Even if those stories can be proved?' asked Maitland gently.

'I don't know what you're talking about.'

'I think you do.'

'There's no-one as'll speak against me.'

'Isn't there?'

'Except this Jim Arnold chap you're talking about. Seems to be to his advantage. But me and my mate have been up to nothing wrong, and there's nobody can say different.'

'Your mate?'

'Never you mind. If you're out to make trouble I'm not getting him into hot water too.'

'I think you mean Stan Bond. He's been with you on your missions, to Fulham, for instance, on the first Monday of every month. And in the evening to a certain block of flats near Earlsfield. You had other districts to cover, of course, which I think could be quite easily established. But I'm not interested in those.'

'I've nothing to say to you.'

'Are you familiar with the phrase, *subpoena*, Mr Gray?' Geoffrey asked.

'No.'

'Having been to prison yourself several times I thought you might be. It's a summons to attend at court and give evidence, and we intend to call you when Jim Arnold is tried. There'll be certain questions asked, by Mr Maitland here, questions which now you seem unwilling to answer. If you refuse then you'll be in contempt of court, and if you answer falsely you'd be liable to a charge of perjury. For a man with your record that could be quite serious.'

'Are you threatening me?' His belt was fastened now and he surged forward threateningly.

'No, Mr Gray. Just pointing out certain facts which you might otherwise ignore to your own detriment.'

'Get out!'

Geoffrey, as it was Antony's habit to describe irreverently to himself, went into his song-and-dance act. 'I'm Mr James Arnold's solicitor,' he said. 'I presume you've heard that he's been arrested.'

'Lawyers, eh?'

'Yes, this is Mr Maitland, his counsel.'

'What am I supposed to know about this James Arnold? Never heard of him.'

Geoffrey ignored this. 'He told us all about your activities in Fulham,' he said, 'and we have discovered enough from other sources to presume that you and Mr Gray were active in other parts of London too. It's my intention to *subpoena* you both to give evidence to that effect.'

'You must be mad.'

'No, I don't think so. As I explained to Mr Gray there's the question of contempt of court if you fail to answer questions. On the other hand if you answer them incorrectly the penalties for perjury are quite severe.'

As he finished speaking Antony became aware that the door had opened and that Mrs Bond was standing there wide eyed. 'Oh Stan!' she said. 'Whatever have you been and got yourself mixed up in? And sitting there in your pyjamas too!'

'Nothing to do with you, woman.'

'It's that job of yours, I knew it. I never trusted that Alf Gray.' She came across the room and put a mug of strong tea down beside him (strong enough to make Antony shudder at the mere sight) and shook some tablets out of a bottle into his outstretched hand. 'You'll feel better when you've had those,' she said, her former taciturnity seemingly forgotten,' and when you've drunk them down you'd better tell these gentlemen what they want to know.' It seemed she had been listening, perhaps for longer than any of them had realised.

Stan put the tablets into his mouth and gulped some of the tea. 'I refuse to answer on the grounds that it might incriminate me,' he said.

Maitland, who all this time had remained quietly in the background, intervened at this point. 'You've been watching American movies on television,' he said. 'I quite agree we've no means of forcing you to answer at this point, and we certainly can't promise you immunity, but if Mr Horton issues a *subpoena* you'll find the results will be just as he described them to you. Besides, he forgot to tell you that you don't have to incriminate yourself, we have evidence that will do it quite effectively without that.'

'There's none of them dare talk,' said Stan, becoming belligerent.

'None of whom?'

'None of them.'

'May we take that as an admission that Jim Arnold wasn't your only victim?'

'Victim?' said Mrs Bond distressfully. 'Oh Stan,' she moaned again.

'You shouldn't grumble. I bring home the money, don't I? It's nothing to do with you how I get it.'

'But if it's all going to come out in court –'

'Nothing of the sort, they're just bluffing.'

'You can believe that if you like, but you'll find out soon enough that you're wrong,' said Maitland. 'Tell him, Geoffrey, tell him exactly what was in that report.'

'The one you wouldn't read?' Horton couldn't resist asking. 'All right then, it's like this, Mr Bond . . .' He went on to describe the result of the enquiry agents' investigations, stressing, as Maitland had insisted, the fact that their only original source of information had been Jim Arnold. Stan was on his feet by the time Geoffrey had finished, and his fists were clenched.

'All right then,' he said. 'What about it? What if I was to do you now?'

'If you mean what I think you mean by that, you'd be laying yourself open to a charge of assault.'

'And it wouldn't do you any good, Mr Bond,' Maitland put in, suppressing with difficulty the vision of Mrs Mopp that Stan's phrase had conjured up. 'To use your own idiom, we're merely Jim Arnold's mouthpieces, the people with the evidence are the enquiry agents we spoke of.'

'All right then, what do you want of me?'

'We want to get to the bottom of this. Mrs Bond spoke of your job. Who employs you?'

'Wait a bit, how's this going to help Jim Arnold?'

82

'That's none of your business. Just take it from me that we want to know.'

'Tell them Stan,' Mrs Bond urged.

'Well, I can't then.' It obviously pleased him to say so. 'I don't know.'

'Come now, Mr Bond, that isn't very likely.'

'Likely or not, it's true.'

'How long have you been' – he glanced at the woman and softened his words – 'employed in this way?'

'Five years, more or less.'

'And how were you, shall we say, recruited for the job?'

'That was Alf's doing. Chap came up to him in a pub from what he told me.'

'Just like that?'

'Oh no, he'd been asking questions of the barman. Knew Alf's name and all that. And when he said there was work for two of us, Alf said he knew someone, and that was me.'

'You yourself never saw the man?'

'No, never.'

'Did your friend Alf describe him to you? Or tell you his name?'

'Said he was oldish, but as for his name I don't think he knew it himself.'

'Come now, that doesn't seem very likely.'

'That's how it was,' Stan insisted. 'We used to get our instructions, quite detailed they were, which shops were doing well and all like that. Told us what we should ask each one to pay, and when we should put the screw on a bit to get some more.'

Mrs Bond, who had long since sunk into one of the rather shabby armchairs, gave a moan at this point and said again, 'Oh Stan,' reminding Antony of nothing so much as a gramophone record that had got stuck in one groove. 'How could you?' she added for good measure.

'It was a living, wasn't it?'

Antony and Geoffrey exchanged a glance and each knew what the other was thinking, that it was probably as well not to stress the fact that two men had died and a fair number of others been seriously injured owing in part to Stan's activities. Almost certainly they'd just be told that it was mainly Alf's doing, but Antony at least had gained the impression that the violent part of their activities had passed altogether from Stan's mind, that the consequences of his actions were the least thing that was bothering him now.

'So you made your collections in a number of different areas?' he asked.

'Twenty in all.' He sounded almost proud of the fact. 'Five days a week for four weeks, and then there'd perhaps be a day or two off. And the pay was good,' he assured the woman. 'You know I've never stinted you.'

'But it would have been even better,' Antony suggested, 'if you and Alf had gone into business on your own, say?'

'Oh, we talked about that, don't you worry. But this chap of his knew the ropes, see. Seemed to do better working for him.'

'Had he any other employees?'

'Not as I knows on, Alf and I thought we were the only two.'

That at least was something to be thankful for. 'And now, as for the disposal of your takings –'

'Come again?'

'You made a collection each day,' said Geoffrey. 'What did you do with the money?'

'Took our cuts, of course.'

'How much was that?'

'It varied. Five percent each, if you must know.'

'And then?'

'Went to this Kenyon Court place, not too far from Earlsfield Station on the Southern Railway, only we didn't always use that. Depended on where we'd been working.'

'And when you got there?'

'Alf had a key the chap had given him. All we had to do was walk into the hall, the main door wasn't locked, unlock a cupboard under the stairs, put in the full briefcase and take out an empty one. Pretty simple really.'

'And how did you receive these detailed instructions you spoke of?'

'Oh, there'd sometimes be a piece of paper in the new briefcase. Alf's a bit of a scholar, he saw to all that.'

'And when you had something to report? That one of your

clients was being recalcitrant perhaps?'

'If someone wouldn't pay up,' said Geoffrey, before Stan could speak. 'Did you ask for instructions as to what to do?'

'Well, we knew. Not that he liked what we did the first time, said the shop should have been messed up too. But he'd no complaints after that.'

'I see.' That was Maitland taking over again. 'Well, I think that's all we have to ask you now, but you do understand – don't you, Mr Bond? – that the game's up, there'll be no more of these collections, no more violence.'

'And who's to stop me? Not you?'

'Certainly not us. The police, I should think.'

'Here now, I've told you what you wanted, now it's your turn to help me.'

'We did explain to you that we couldn't promise you immunity.' ('Oh, Stan,' said the gramophone record in the background.) 'But I think you'll find, if you're willing to tell what you know, that it may go easier with you.'

'And what do I say to Alf?'

'That's another matter. If I were you I'd keep well out of his way. In fact,' said Antony, suddenly inspired, 'why don't you come with us now to the nearest police station and make a statement?'

'I don't like the sound of that.'

'No, Mr Bond.' Geoffrey had been thinking things over. 'If you're afraid of your friend, and don't think I blame you, I should just tell him that we questioned you and you told us nothing. Then he'll have no grudge against you later on.'

'He'll know if I give evidence at this trial you're talking about.'

'It may never come to that,' said Antony soothingly. 'If we can lay our hands on your employer –' But he added to Geoffrey, as they walked away from the little house a few minutes later, 'I don't see how we're going to do that.'

'Then we shall *subpoena* both Alf and Stan,' said Geoffrey prosaically. And added with a grin, 'And Mrs Bond will probably come along too as a sort of Greek chorus.' He paused there, in fact he came to a complete halt, and gave Antony a searching look. 'You've got some idea in your head,' he said accusingly.

85

'An idea, a vague idea,' Maitland told him. 'And for all the good it will do us . . . damn all, I expect.'

'So the next thing is to go to the police?'

'Let's talk to Don Tudor first, because I promised him I wouldn't do anything to get him into trouble with these characters. But when he hears what I have to say I'm pretty sure he'll give me the go-ahead.'

'How are you going to set about it?'

'I shall see Sykes. I know it isn't strictly his pigeon, but he'll set the wheels in motion. If Stan's right and there were only the two involved in the actual collection that should effectively put a stop to things, for the time being at any rate.'

'Do you think Stan will stay there quietly waiting to be arrested?'

'Oh, I should think so. It will take him the rest of the day to explain himself to his wife – common law – whom I suspect of being a rather stronger character than she would appear on the surface. And, you know, I don't think he's really conscious of exactly how serious the position is for him.'

'What about Alf then?'

'He knows all right, but I think he's too vain to think we can do anything to harm him. We shall see, anyway. I'll talk to Don Tudor and then to Sykes, and that's all we can do for the moment.'

'What exactly do you mean by that, Antony?'

'Just what I say. Why will no-one ever believe me?'

'Because we know you,' said Geoffrey bluntly. 'You've got some idea in your head as to which of the men at Kenyon Court may be involved and I expect you mean to go on from there. And he's a man, let me remind you, who hasn't turned a hair at murder.'

'Murder done by somebody else. By the time I get round to making any further enquiries Alf and Stan won't be available to do his dirty work for him. Besides, Geoffrey, you needn't worry just yet. If I could think of any questions to ask these people . . . but at the moment I can't.'

'That won't last,' Geoffrey predicted. 'All right, Antony, I'll take you home and you can go on with your programme, but don't forget to let me know when you need me again.'

Antony grinned at him. 'My dear instructing solicitor,' he said, 'surely it's you who should be getting in touch with me.'

II

Maitland took a circuitous route home through Fulham. Both sides
of the Tudors' shop were busy that morning, but he succeeded in
extricating the owners temporarily and received enthusiastic
endorsement for his proposal from Mavis, and a less willing agreement from Don. Armed with this he went home, commandeered
the telephone, and ran Chief Inspector Sykes to earth eventually at
his home. Jenny, meanwhile, had gone downstairs to explain his
lateness for their usual Saturday luncheon. Antony was still
inclined to be formal with Vera, though he knew well enough that
she would make no objection; as for Sir Nicholas his undutiful
nephew would have said that adversity – in the form of being kept
waiting for the meal – was good for his uncle's soul.

Sykes had to be fetched in from the garden where he was raking
leaves. As was his habit, he would have started their conversation
with the usual polite enquiries as to everyone's health, had Antony
not interrupted him impatiently. 'Concerning our talk the other
day,' he said.

There was a moment's silence. 'Are you wanting some more
information, Mr Maitland?' Sykes asked cautiously.

'No, I've got some for you. The names and addresses of the two
men engaged in the protection racket as collectors and strongarm
men.'

'Is this more information from your client?'

'It's based on what he told us. But I don't particularly want his
name mentioned.'

'You're asking me to take his word on trust?'

'No, not at all. There's a copy of a report from Cobbolds . . . you
know them, Chief Inspector, they're a very respectable outfit,
Geoffrey Horton always uses them . . . that should tell you if you
didn't know already.'

'I've heard of them, Mr Maitland.'

'Well, if you'll tell me who to pass the word to I'll do so, but I
think some action should be taken quickly. Can you arrange that?'

'I take it that means you've alerted both men?'

'Geoffrey and I went to see them in the normal course of
preparing Jim Arnold's defence. That couldn't be avoided, because

87

the merchants they'd been bleeding dry are much too afraid to talk. Only one . . . and if you think I'm going to give you his name you're wrong. But the point is, threats have been made against his wife, and I expect that has been done in other cases too.'

'Do these two men know who informed against them?'

'Only that what Jim told us enabled us to put enquiries in hand.'

'You'd better give me their names.'

Antony did so. 'I understand they've both got records,' he added, 'but it's all in the report. You'll find Alf Gray a tough nut to crack and I think – though I may be wrong about this – that he hasn't enough imagination to realise that what Geoffrey and I know may cause trouble for him. Stan Bond's another matter, and he has his wife to contend with. He finally talked quite freely but we advised him not to let Alf know he'd done so. If some misguided magistrate lets them out on bail –'

'Yes, I take your point. Am I to take it these two were the only men concerned?'

'As far as I know the only men concerned as collectors. They worked for a man whom Stan says he never saw and whose name he doesn't know, who gave them explicit directions as to who to victimise and how much money to demand from each. I think he'll be just as voluble to your colleagues as he was to us, Chief Inspector.'

'And you don't know who this man is?'

'I do not.'

'It's not like you to be so helpful, Mr Maitland,' said Sykes bluntly.

Antony laughed. 'I think you're wronging me, but I admit in this case I have my reasons. Will you look after it for me, or tell me what I should do?'

'I'll look after it. Where's this report now?'

'I have a copy here. If you could send someone round to Kempenfeldt Square for it I'll put it in an envelope and leave it with Gibbs.'

'I think that can be managed. You say you've no idea –'

'I said I didn't know, Chief Inspector.' As might have been expected Sykes argued a little after that, but Maitland was adamant and after a while was able to ring off. After a little rummaging he found an envelope large enough to take the report. He went down to join the rest of his family, not too dissatisfied with the morning's work.

III

Gibbs, when he handed over his envelope, received it with ill grace and the comment that it wasn't very nice to have members of the constabulary calling at the house. 'Will you ask Sir Nicholas if I may serve luncheon now, Mr Maitland?' he added in a not-too-subtle reproof, to which Antony replied, 'Give us a quarter of an hour and then go ahead, Gibbs,' which he hoped would accord well enough with everyone's wishes.

Sir Nicholas on the other hand made no immediate comment on his lateness and then only obliquely. First he provided his nephew with sherry and then said, going back to his own chair, 'Jenny tells us you've suffered no ill effects from interviewing these two rather rough characters this morning.'

'I told you, Uncle Nick, I'd have Geoffrey with me.'

'I have every respect for Geoffrey, but have never considered him particularly suitable as a bodyguard,' said Sir Nicholas rather austerely.

'I shouldn't be surprised if you underrate him. But that wasn't exactly what I meant, as I think you know. He did his best to terrorise them with the majesty of the law, and one of them – this chap called Stan Bond – was actually scared enough to talk to us. Prompted by his wife . . . common law.'

'Which conversation you have passed on to Chief Inspector Sykes?'

'Yes, I expect Jenny told you that too. Part of what Stan told us, and Cobbolds' report.'

'Not altogether wise to play games with the police,' said Vera in her gruff way.

'If you mean that I didn't waste time telling him everything, Vera, it wasn't exactly playing games,' Antony explained. 'It's all in Cobbolds' report. Only I thought if we got talking about Kenyon Court he might press me for my opinion, and it's far too nebulous to be anything but slanderous at this stage.'

'Antony has an idea,' said Jenny brightly, 'but he won't even tell me what it is.'

'Guesswork,' said Sir Nicholas dampingly. 'Am I to take it, Antony, that you're proposing to take this matter further?'

'If I can see my way. Come now, Uncle Nick, you must see there's absolutely no danger once Alf and Stan are out of the way. This chap doesn't do his own dirty work.'

'Something in that,' said Vera. 'And I see it's already occurred to Jenny.'

'I hope you're all right, but I fail to see how you propose to set about it, Antony. Don't you really think you've done enough for Jim Arnold?' asked Sir Nicholas.

'I know we can make up a pretty good tale on what we've got, and probably get him off with a lighter sentence. But that's not all I want, Uncle Nick.'

'We know the money went to Kenyon Court. That in itself will provide you with some ammunition, some reason for him choosing that place when he needed money.'

'Yes, of course. But there's the publicity angle . . . remember?'

'Your part in it, Nicholas,' Vera reminded her husband.

'Which I have the gravest doubts of being able to perform successfully. Not that I shouldn't like to help Jim Arnold,' said Sir Nicholas, relenting, 'but such influence as I am able to bring to bear may not be enough.'

'I think it would be, Uncle Nick,' said Jenny. 'I knew of someone who wanted to go to Canada, a friend of Peter and Nan, but she was separated from her husband and didn't know where he was and that caused difficulties. When she went to their office over here the man at the counter said "That will have to be referred to Ottawa," and then the man in charge wouldn't do it.'

'That story, my dear, is hardly a parallel.'

'No, of course it isn't, but what I was going to say is that the woman concerned wrote to her MP, and he did whatever MPs do on these occasions and eventually it *was* referred to Ottawa and Ottawa said yes. So I think if Antony makes a good enough story of it —'

'And particularly if the press take it up,' said Antony.

'That ever I should live to see this day,' his uncle remarked to the room at large, but Jenny was intent on her story and ignored him.

'I did something about that this morning, Antony,' she said. 'I talked to Clare Charlton, and told her I'd let her know when the trial was coming on and she was to make sure Harry attended it. He'd make a good dramatic tale out of all this.'

'So long as he understands he's got to arouse sympathy for Jim.'

'Oh yes, I made that quite clear to Clare. Don't you think it was a good idea?' said Jenny anxiously.

'Very good, love. But the trouble is, you see,' said Antony, look-ing from Sir Nicholas to Vera, 'I'd like to talk to all these people in Kenyon Court – except Henry Franklin, of course – but I can't think of any excuse for doing so.'

'Unfortunately I've no doubt your ingenuity will prove equal to the task,' said Sir Nicholas. 'And I agree, of course, that having this knowledge it was your clear duty to hand it over to the police. But why to Sykes?'

'It seemed the easiest way. Even though it isn't his department he'd know exactly who should deal with it.'

'That's so. I suppose he knows why you're interesting yourself in this matter.'

'Yes, he knows that.'

'Then what I should like to know, my dear boy – and I hope you'll ask him if the opportunity arises – is what his superior, Chief Superintendent Briggs, thinks of your latest client.'

'Oh, come now, Uncle Nick, this has nothing to do with Briggs.'

'I seem to have heard you say something like that before, when you were acting above and beyond the call of duty, as people are far too fond of saying nowadays. That didn't prevent certain – shall we say? – unpleasantnesses arising.'

'Got to remember that, Antony,' said Vera. 'Nicholas is right, Briggs has had some very odd ideas about you in the past.'

'Such as suspecting you of faking evidence,' her husband put in.

'Yes, but don't you see' – Antony glanced at Jenny, across whose serenity a faint cloud was appearing – 'he'll never think that in this case. It wouldn't be worth my while to rig the evidence unless some cash was involved, and Jim Arnold couldn't afford to pay me.'

At that point, perhaps fortunately, Gibbs arrived to say that luncheon was served. The manilla envelope was still on the hall table when they went across to the dining-room, but Antony passed it without a glance. Already Alf and Stan were fading from his mind, all his thoughts were focussed on their employer, and on the problem of gaining access to the people at Kenyon Court.

But that was something that was to be solved in a way he didn't expect, and that he couldn't possibly have foreseen.

IV

The Maitlands' closest friends were Roger and Meg Farrell, and as Meg was an actress, better known to the theatre-going public as Margaret Hamilton, Roger was often at a loose end in the evening and was in the habit of dropping in at Kempenfeldt Square and staying until it was time to fetch Meg from the theatre. That evening he had been dining with Antony and Jenny, and when the phone rang almost as soon as they had finished dinner he and Jenny went on clearing the table while Antony went to answer it. His first feeling when he heard Sykes's voice was one of astonish-ment, but then he thought that probably the detective's punctilious nature had prompted him to express his thanks for the tip he had received earlier in the day. It was therefore with complete surprise that he heard the other man's voice, more serious than usual, say, 'The Chief Superintendent would like to see you, Mr Maitland.'

'Briggs?' The question came sharply. Then he recovered himself. 'There are two sides to that, Chief Inspector,' he pointed out, 'I don't think I have the faintest desire to see *him*.'

'I hope you'll reconsider that.'

'Why should I?'

'Because he wants to know exactly what you know about Kenyon Court.'

'I told you —'

'On the contrary, Mr Maitland, you never mentioned the place. If you had the connection would have been made sooner.'

'I don't understand you, what connection?'

'Between the protection racket which you claim to have solved

92

in part, and a case I'm working on.'

'I still don't understand, I'm afraid.'

'It's really quite simple.'

'I suppose you mean ... a murder?' He made the words a question.

'Of course I do, and, as you know, I report to the Chief Superintendent.'

'But what the hell has it to do with me?'

'Because the murdered woman, Mr Maitland, is a Mrs Joyce Prior, who lived in Flat One in Kenyon Court. She seems to have been poisoned at a gathering of all the tenants last night in the owner's flat. At least, that's where she was taken ill. If you'd been more open with me –'

'I was hiding nothing, it was all in the report.'

'Yes, I know that. Still, the connection would have been made earlier. In the circumstances, Mr Maitland,' Sykes went on, 'I don't think you can be altogether surprised that Chief Superintendent Briggs wants to see you.'

When Antony turned from the telephone a few moments later he found that both Jenny and Roger had abandoned their task and were listening unashamedly. 'What is it?' asked Jenny anxiously. 'What's happened now?'

'A death,' said Antony slowly. 'A murder, to be more precise, for which I'm afraid I must take some of the responsibility.'

'That's nonsense,' said Roger.

'I'm not so sure. You're up-to-date on the Jim Arnold affair, Roger –'

'I had the final instalment just before dinner, with you both speaking in chorus,' said Roger smiling.

'Exactly. Well, the dead woman is one of the inhabitants of Kenyon Court.'

'How did she die? And what is it to do with you?' Jenny demanded.

'I don't know the details, but she died of poisoning apparently. Sykes said – you gathered it was Chief Inspector Sykes on the phone? – that the first effects made themselves noticed at a – a gathering I think he called it, called by their landlord last night. I have a nasty feeling that it must be the direct result of my talking to Rita Franklin, who is the owner's wife. If somebody realised that the search for the man responsible for the protection racket had been narrowed down to that building –'

'You didn't tell this Mrs Franklin that, I imagine,' said Roger.

'No, of course I didn't, but she's by no means an idiot and she guessed I was particularly interested in the people there.'

'Even so, why murder this – this Mrs Prior? You said one of the chaps you interviewed today had been recruited by a man.'

'Yes, that's true. I can only think that somehow or other she knew too much.'

'That would mean . . . her husband?' said Jenny, thinking it out as she went. 'He's the man who's away so much, isn't he? And you said – or was it Uncle Nick or Vera? – that if he were involved his wife must be an active accomplice.'

'Jenny love that's a remarkably lucid statement, coming from you.'

'But I'm right, aren't I?'

'Quite right. Archie Prior . . . Archibald I suppose. But if he couldn't trust her, why did he confide in her in the first place?'

'Things change in marriages,' said Jenny wisely. 'If they'd quarrelled, that would make a difference, wouldn't it?'

'It certainly would, but it still doesn't explain,' said Roger, 'why he should go to this party . . . this gathering . . . prepared to poison her. After all you didn't see his two accomplices until today, he could have had no reason to be afraid until he heard what Mrs Franklin had to say.'

'We're all assuming he did it, and on the face of it it does seem the most reasonable thing. As for going prepared, the same objection applies to everybody else. Unless, of course, it was Henry Franklin himself. And Sykes didn't actually say she was poisoned at the party, only that she was taken ill there. It all depends how quick-acting a poison was used.'

'Perhaps you'll know that when you've talked to the police,' said Jenny. 'Uncle Nick isn't going to like it, is he, Antony? What did you arrange about that?'

'I said – you must have heard me – that I was damned if I was going to Scotland Yard at this time of night. After all, it's not as if I was suspected of anything. But they could come here if they liked, and they'd better ask for Uncle Nick. I'm going down now and I'll send Vera up to join you. Then after Sykes and Briggs have gone he can speak his mind without inhibition, and we can all get back to the business of living again.'

'I think that's wise,' said Jenny. 'If there's one thing Uncle Nick hates it's being kept in the dark,' she added to Roger, who already knew it well enough. 'But —'

'I know what you're thinking, love, it isn't customary for Chief Superintendents to take a hand themselves in a matter like this.'

'No, I've always thought of them like spiders sitting at the centre of the web and . . . what's the word, Antony?'

It was Roger who supplied it. 'Collating evidence. But you haven't explained —'

'It's quite simple,' said Maitland. 'He's taking a hand himself because I'm involved. You know all about that, Roger, we've had enough trouble with him in the past.'

'Yes, but —'

'It's nothing to worry about. Heaven knows what frightfulness he's suspecting me of this time, but I haven't anything on my conscience so I needn't worry.'

All the same, as he went downstairs a few moments later he was very well aware that, as far as Jenny was concerned at least, his words had fallen on deaf ears. She wasn't a worrier by nature but he certainly had the knack of disturbing that serenity of hers that he valued so much.

V

As it turned out there was plenty of time for explanations before the two detectives arrived. Sir Nicholas was scowling by the time his nephew had finished. 'This propensity of yours for involving yourself with the law —' he was beginning when Vera interrupted him.

'Not Antony's fault,' she said flatly.

'You will pardon me, my dear, for contradicting you, but if he hadn't behaved like an imbecile the first time he came into contact with Chief Superintendent Briggs, none of this would have

95

happened.' (The antagonism between the two men was of long standing, and on both sides quite easily explained. On Antony's it was an instinctive dislike that had increased over the years; but Briggs quite simply distrusted him, and appeared ready to attribute any or all of the crimes in the calendar to his door.'

'Can't be helped now,' said Vera. 'And I think I shall stay for this interview. After all, you can hardly turn me out of my own drawing-room.' She looked around her with some pleasure. 'Not a drawing-room exactly,' she added, with her instinct for precision – they were sitting in the study as usual – 'but it comes to the same thing.'

'Stay by all means, my dear,' said Sir Nicholas cordially. 'Perhaps between the two of us we may be able to prevent any excess of stupidity on Antony's part.'

'You needn't worry, Vera,' Antony told her. 'The murder doesn't concern me or any of my clients so I've nothing whatever to hide, even from Briggs. And if in the course of our talk I succeeded in persuading one of them to tell us a little more about what's happened . . . well, that's all to the good, isn't it?'

'Answer their questions and don't add a thing of your own,' his uncle advised him. But Antony only smiled at that and declined to commit himself.

At ten o'clock, when the visitors hadn't arrived, Antony pulled the study door ajar so that they might hear the front door bell. On the whole it was as well that Gibbs would have retired, he'd been known to refer to even the most senior of police officers as persons, and if anything had been needed to increase Briggs's animosity, it would have been to be announced in this way. No sooner had Antony done so, and noticed with some relief that the butler was missing from his chosen lurking place, than the bell did ring and he went to answer it himself.

Briggs surged in first, a big man, a good deal overweight, with a bald head and a highly coloured complexion that made Antony wonder sometimes whether he had a tendency to apoplexy. Following, Sykes, though certainly not a small man either in height or breadth of shoulder, had rather the air of a tug working its way into position beside a liner. 'Well, Mr Maitland,' said Briggs ominously, 'we meet again.'

Antony suppressed the instinct to reply in kind, or even to point out that the remark was hardly original. 'Good evening, Superintendent . . . Chief Inspector,' he said. 'I have to tell you I don't altogether understand the urgent necessity for this meeting, but of course I'm very glad to help in any way I can.' He saw a rather sardonic look come over Sykes's face, and went on in a hurry, 'Come into the study. My uncle and aunt – have you met Lady Harding, Chief Superintendent? – are interested to know what you have to say.'

'Feeling a little need for moral support?' asked Briggs with something approaching a sneer. It was nearly six months since the two men had actually met, and then it had been in court when Briggs, much against his will, had been called for the defence in a case where Maitland was appearing. It was quite obvious that the memory of that encounter still rankled.

'Not at all,' said Antony airily, 'but you must allow us all a little natural curiosity. Your request for a meeting was so extraordinary –'

'In the circumstances, Mr Maitland, I think it was very natural,' Sykes put in pacifically. The house was well known to him and he began to urge his superior officer down the hall. 'I'm sure there can be no objection to Sir Nicholas and Lady Harding hearing what we have to say. You remember, sir,' he added to Briggs, 'that Lady Harding was a barrister herself before her marriage.'

Briggs didn't deign to reply to that, but allowed himself to be steered into the study. His greeting to its occupants was slightly more orthodox than the one he had accorded to their nephew, but there was no doubting his annoyance and Vera exchanged the nearest she could manage to an impish grin with Antony before they all seated themselves. It was Briggs who opened the attack. 'This statement from a firm of enquiry agents which you were instrumental in having handed over to the police, Mr Maitland. Why was it obtained?'

'My instructing solicitor, Geoffrey Horton, could tell you more about that, Chief Superintendent, since the investigation was made on his instructions, in the course of preparing the defence of one of our clients.'

'Which one?'

Sykes had indeed carried discretion to its utmost length, but there was nothing for it now but complete frankness. 'A man called Jim Arnold,' Antony said. 'He's been a client of mine for a long time, on and off –'

'You're telling me he has a record.'

'Yes, but since he came out of prison about seven years ago he's been going straight.'

'Then why is he your client now?'

'Until now, I should have said. He was arrested for attempting to steal a valuable collection of coins from Henry Franklin, the owner of Kenyon Court.'

'Caught red-handed,' put in Sykes *sotto voce*.

'Oh, I admit it, Chief Inspector, but there are extenuating circumstances and I'm entitled to point them out to the court. I won't bore you with the whole story –'

'You certainly won't bore me, Mr Maitland, but I want the full truth,' said Briggs roughly.

'The truth but not the full truth,' Antony amended. 'That, I think, I'm entitled to keep to myself. But I'll tell you this much, he'd been paying protection money for years, and had discovered by doing a little detective work himself that the money was being delivered to Kenyon Court, though as the men who collected it knew him by sight he wasn't able to follow them in and find out to which of the flats they went.'

'According to this statement from Cobbolds it wasn't delivered to a flat at all.'

'No, I know that, but I'm trying to answer you as I understood the matter then. You see, Arnold needed money, and because of the way he'd been victimised he was very short of it, so I'm afraid his mind turned to his old trade again. So he thought the matter over and decided that the ground floor at Kenyon Court was the most likely place for the money to be delivered, and of the two couples living there probably the owner was the more likely to be involved. In that way, then, he felt that he was merely getting his own back, in the literal sense I mean.'

'His choice of the Franklins' flat wouldn't have anything to do with the fact that Mr Franklin, as the retired owner of an antique shop, might be expected to have more valuables about?' asked

98

Sykes cynically.

'You should guard against it, Chief Inspector. I've heard before that the police are apt to develop nasty suspicious minds.'

'Never mind that,' snapped Briggs. 'I'd like to know what your interest is in this James Arnold.'

'I'm s-sorry for him,' said Maitland simply, but the first hint of the angry, betraying stammer was enough to make Sir Nicholas and Vera exchange anxious glances.

'Yes, I know that sympathetic nature of yours.'

'You're sneering again, Chief Superintendent, and you don't do it very well. If you want to take it up I'd practise in front of a mirror,' said Antony with intent to annoy, and watched with some satisfaction the crimson hue of Briggs's countenance turn slowly purple.

'But your researches didn't end there,' said Sykes quickly, before the other detective could speak.

'No,' said Antony. 'I saw both the men concerned, the collectors, as I told you, Chief Inspector. What has happened about them by the way?'

'That is not a matter within our jurisdiction,' said Briggs, finding his voice again.

'All the same, it would be interesting to know who their principal is.'

'We think so too,' said Sykes, 'but they both profess ignorance, as you probably know. But what I think the Chief Superintendent is interested in, Mr Maitland, is the call you paid yesterday on Mrs Rita Franklin.'

'Was there any reason why I shouldn't call on her?'

'She could hardly help you with your enquiries,' said Briggs flatly.

'On the c-contrary I found her both helpful and s-sympathetic.'

'Sympathetic towards the man who robbed her husband?'

'Perhaps that wasn't the right way to put it. But she wasn't obstructive.'

'What did you hope to learn from her?' Briggs had taken over again and his tone was sharp.

'Something about the other people who live in the same b-building.'

99

'I can't see why that should concern you. I presume you mean, in order to find out who the man behind the protection racket is.'

'Of c-course I mean that, and it's very much my b-business.'

'You'll forgive us, Mr Maitland, if that seems a little obscure to us,' said Sykes. 'You have your report, which was very properly turned over to the police, wouldn't that be enough to base your extenuating circumstances on?'

'The defence would be so much more effective if the principal could be named . . . don't you think?'

'Perhaps so. Is that how you put it to Mrs Franklin?'

'Of course not. I told her a story that I hoped would conceal my interest, but I'm afraid she didn't swallow it.'

'Not very discreet of you, was it?' said Briggs.

'Perhaps n-not.'

'I should like a complete account of your talk together.'

'I think I can give you that.' He cast his mind back for a moment before beginning, and then told the tale lucidly enough. 'So you see,' he concluded, 'she must have done a little putting two and two together after I left. She guessed my interest in the people in the house, I knew that already; perhaps later she guessed the line our defence of Jim Arnold was going to take. In any event –'

'In any event, it seems she told her husband about your visit when he came in, enough to make him anxious.'

'If he had a guilty conscience that would be very natural,' said Antony lightly. He was putting up a pretty good fight to keep his temper.

'Yes, but in that case why should he have called a meeting of all his tenants?'

'To plan their mutual defence perhaps. It may have been a concerted effort – the protection racket, I mean – with all of them taking a share,' said Antony, improvising freely and watching Briggs's scowl grow blacker. For the moment he had no time to waste on his uncle's and aunt's reactions.

'It isn't a laughing matter, Mr Maitland,' said Sykes mildly. He was concerned, as Antony knew well enough, to prevent an open clash between the two men.

'I'm not laughing, it's a theory I think should appeal to the Chief Superintendent.' He paused hopefully, but no comment was forthcoming. 'Well, if you won't tell me what's happened to Alf Gray and Stan Bond you won't –'

'They're both under arrest,' Sykes told him.

'Cobbolds' observations by themselves were not exactly proof of any wrongdoing,' Antony pointed out.

'Bond talked.'

'I see. Will you answer one more question for me? Have you asked Henry Franklin who rented the cupboard under the stairs as extra storage space?'

Sykes didn't even glance at his superior. He'd always been a man who took his own way, and though he might seem ready with the information, Antony knew well enough that he had his own reasons for imparting it. 'That was almost the first question we asked him,' he said. 'So far as he knows there was only one key, and he gave it to Mrs Joyce Prior who said she wanted to keep some antique pieces there that she picked up on her own account for resale.'

'The woman who was murdered?'

'Quite so.'

'And where was the money collected on Friday?'

'Where would you expect? Still in the cupboard.'

'How did she die?'

'One of the synthetic analgesics we believe,' said Sykes, and for the first time seemed to notice the Chief Superintendent fuming beside him. 'You can get any other information you want from the morning paper, Mr Maitland,' he pointed out. 'Meanwhile we'd like to know what you've discovered about the person who employed Gray and Bond. I think I've some right now to ask the question, as it seems obvious that the two things must be connected.'

'It seems obvious to me too, Chief Inspector, but I can't help you. I haven't thought of an excuse yet to approach the other people who live in Kenyon Court, but I'll tell you one thing, I don't think Mrs Prior could have been in it alone.'

'Come now, Mr Maitland,' – Briggs too seemed to have forgotten Sir Nicholas's presence – 'where's this celebrated intuition we've all heard so much about ? Surely you've obtained some hint from all these enquiries you've been making?'

'My enquiries of necessity fell short of those you will make Chief Superintendent,' Antony pointed out. 'If you haven't c-come up with the answer, why should you expect that I have?'

'There's been very little time,' Briggs retorted, 'but I've come to you because I know your ways. You'd stop at nothing to win this case of yours –'

He broke off as Sir Nicholas rose to his feet in his leisurely way. 'I must thank you for letting us sit in on your discussion, Chief Superintendent,' he said, stressing the word a little, 'but I think you'll agree this has gone far enough. My nephew has been very open with you, perhaps more open than his client's interest should have dictated.'

'In a case of murder we've every right to expect co-operation.'

'Precisely. I'm sure that thought has guided him. But now you'll forgive me, Chief Superintendent, it's getting late and quite frankly I must ask you to regard the matter as closed.'

Briggs was on his feet too, his eyes almost level with Sir Nicholas's. 'We'll see about that,' he said. 'One of these days this precious nephew of yours will go too far and then we'll see who has the last laugh.' He turned on his heel as he spoke and was through the doorway before any of them could speak. Sykes followed, turning to shrug apologetically before he too disappeared.

'I hope you're satisfied,' said Sir Nicholas bitterly to Antony.

'On the contrary,' said Antony, as dulcetly as his uncle himself might have done when he was really annoyed, 'it's you who should be congratulated, Uncle Nick. Don't you think so, Vera? On my own I could never have routed Briggs so completely.'

'That silenced him just long enough for me to get away,' he told Jenny and Roger later, when he had finished recounting the meeting with the two detectives. 'But unless Vera can calm him down in the meantime, he'll have more to say about it tomorrow, you can be sure of that. With particular reference to the fact,' he added remorsefully, 'that I only barely held on to my temper.'

I

Sunday had passed quietly, with Antony more silent than usual, Sir Nicholas holding his fire, and Vera and Jenny – along with Meg and Roger when they arrived at tea-time – making rather frantic conversation to cover the gap. By the time he arrived in chambers on Monday morning Maitland was no nearer to solving his problem, and had almost made up his mind to go to Kenyon Court at the first opportunity, and trust to the inspiration of the moment for an excuse for his presence. He had no sooner shut the outer door behind him, however, than John Willett burst out of the clerks' office.

'You're wanted on the telephone, Mr Maitland,' he said.

Willett was junior only to old Mr Mallory now, and had always taken an especial interest in Antony's affairs, partly because he had got the job through him in the first place. Officially Mr Mallory had power of life and death over the work that came into chambers, but over the years the younger clerk had discovered his own ways of circumventing the old man when his decisions seemed to be likely to go against Maitland's wishes. Now there was an air of excitement about him, but as this was not unusual Antony discounted it. Willett was a man who never walked when he could run, and whose natural mode of expression was rather breathless.

'You know I'm due in court,' said Maitland rather brusquely. 'Get the caller's name and tell him I'll ring back.'

'It's still quite early,' said Willett firmly. 'I've got all your books and papers ready, we can get there with time to spare. And I really do think you should take this call, Mr Maitland, it's from a Mr Prior.'

It took Antony a moment's thought to make the connection, even though the matter had been so much on his mind. 'Archibald Prior?' he said incredulously.

'That's right. Hill was telling him if he wanted to consult you he'd have to do so through his solicitor.'

'Well so he should, but —'

'That's just what I thought,' said Willett triumphantly. 'I heard Hill address him by name, and in view of what the papers had to say this morning I thought you'd be interested. There's a full ten minutes before we need leave, so won't you take the call?'

'All right,' said Antony, not too reluctantly. 'Tell Hill to put it through to my room.'

Prior had a deep and rather pleasant voice. 'I need your help, Mr Maitland,' he said abruptly as soon as Antony had identified himself.

'I'd be glad to do anything I can, but — I think my clerk explained this to you — you should consult a solicitor first. He may or may not recommend you to come to me.'

'If I was employing him he'd have to do what I wanted, wouldn't he?' asked Prior reasonably, but not at all as if he was sure of the answer. 'Perhaps you could recommend somebody.'

'Haven't you a solicitor of your own?'

'No. My wife dealt with all business matters, and I dare say she gave our lease to somebody to look over, she didn't tell me, but I've never had occasion to consult one.'

Antony nearly said, not even to make a will? but decided in time that the question in the circumstances might not be in the best of taste. 'I was very sorry to hear what had happened to Mrs Prior,' he said formally. 'But if the matter is urgent couldn't you look through her papers and find this man's name?'

'No, I don't think so. I know she was in touch with someone more recently, but that was about the divorce.'

'Divorce?' asked Antony a little startled, and wondering for a moment whether Jenny was developing second sight.

'Look here, Mr Maitland, if you really insist on going about it this way couldn't you tell me the name of the solicitor who's acting for the man who robbed Henry Franklin?'

'Yes, I could do that. His name is Geoffrey Horton, and the firm is Horton, Stanley and Company, with offices at 16 Temple Mews.'

'If I get in touch with him do you think he'll take me on?'

'I don't see why not. But tell me, Mr Prior, what made you pick on me?'

104

'That was Rita Franklin. You came to see her about the burglary, and you seem to have made quite an impression on her. Besides, of course, I do read the papers when I'm at home, so I'd heard of you already.'

'I see.' Perhaps it was as well that at that moment the prospective client couldn't see counsel's face. 'Well, Mr Prior, I'm due in court at the moment, so I'd advise you to get in touch with Mr Horton and see what he suggests.' But he couldn't help adding, his curiosity getting the better of his discretion, 'You haven't told me why you feel the need for legal advice.'

'Because the police seem to think I killed my wife,' said Prior.

The obvious response to that was, and did you? but though Maitland might well have asked it if he'd been face to face with the other man, over the telephone he had certain scruples. He said therefore, rather lamely, 'Oh, I see.' And then, 'Geoffrey Horton would certainly be a good person to talk to in that case.'

'If you're wondering whether I did it,' said Prior – was that a natural question to ask, was he a mind reader, or did it argue some degree of guilt? – 'I didn't!'

'In that case you've probably nothing to worry about.'

'That's what you think,' Prior retorted. 'I'll phone Mr Horton right away,' he added, 'and let you get on with your work.' And rang off without further ado.

It was rather later than usual when the court adjourned for the day, but in spite of Willett's offer to take his things back to chambers Antony decided to accompany him there. And sure enough they were met with a message that a conference had been arranged with Mr Horton and a lay client, and they could be expected in half an hour. Mr Mallory, who seemed to be expecting an explosion of some kind over the arrangement, was obviously taken aback when the news was received calmly. Maitland made his way to his uncle's room, saying over his shoulder, 'I'll be with Sir Nicholas when Mr Horton arrives.'

The battlefield on Sir Nicholas's desk was worse than ever, but he looked up and removed his glasses when his nephew went in. Antony crossed the room and began mechanically to sort out the tangle of papers, saying without preamble, 'The police think Archibald Prior murdered his wife. He and Geoffrey will be here very shortly.'

A barrister's memory can be one of his chief assets, and Sir Nicholas had no difficulty in identifying the name. 'And you're all agog to plunge into the matter,' he said, 'without the faintest idea whether he's innocent or guilty.'

'He says he didn't do it.'

'Good gracious, Antony, if you're going to start taking your clients' word for anything they may choose to tell you –'

'No, Uncle Nick, I've got an open mind. But don't you see, this will give me an opportunity to get near the people at Kenyon Court. I haven't any details yet about this famous gathering, as Sykes calls it, but I understand they were all there.'

'Have you considered the question of conflict of interest?'

'It wouldn't be a conflict,' Antony protested. 'Anything I can discover through taking Pr or on as a client could only help Jim.'

'I knew you were assuming Prior was innocent,' said Sir Nicholas in a resigned tone. 'What if he's the man behind the extortion? Once you're committed to his defence . . . I'd advise you to be very careful how you set about this, Antony.'

'I shall be, but I can't possibly make up my mind until I've seen him.'

'If I know you, you won't be certain even then. But you have this tendency . . . Halloran has often said to me that you're a natural defence lawyer. You want to believe the best of your clients.'

'It's paid off once or twice,' said Antony mildly. 'But you're not really worried about Prior's guilt or innocence, are you, Uncle Nick? It's this business of it being a case that Briggs is ultimately responsible for.'

'That too had crossed my mind,' Sir Nicholas acknowledged. 'I wish I could get you to take that as seriously as Vera and I do, Antony.'

'Just because he's paranoid on the subject there's no need for me to become so to,' said Antony, realising as he spoke that this was not the most diplomatic remark he could have made. In fact Sir Nicholas was only too obviously prepared to flatten him with some devastating come-back when the phone rang to announce that Mr Horton and a Mr Prior were waiting in Maitland's room.

'I'll see you later, Uncle Nick,' said Antony hastily and did his best to ignore his uncle's rather ominous riposte, 'You will indeed' which followed him out of the room.

Maitland's own room was an inconvenient shape, long and rather narrow, and even on a sunny day inclined to be gloomy. By now, of course, the light was on and he switched on the lamp on the desk for good measure before taking stock of Geoffrey's companion. Archibald Prior looked younger than Rita Franklin's description had led him to expect, a tallish, thin man with receding hair, and a vagueness of manner that had not been evident over the telephone. Geoffrey effected introductions, making no refer- ence to the telephone conversation between Prior and Maitland earlier in the day, about which he probably – being a man who took his profession seriously – felt that least said was soonest mended. Antony went round behind the desk, waved the others to chairs, seated himself and said, 'Well now?' questioningly.

Geoffrey, as was proper, took up the challenge. 'You probably read in the papers,' he said, 'of the death of the late Mrs Joyce Prior. The police are looking on it as a case of murder, and Mr Prior feels he has some reason to believe that they suspect him. He tells me they're mistaken.'

'Yes, I see.' He paused a moment, considering. Geoffrey was as wise as he was, because he'd briefed him on the telephone on Sunday morning about the visit that Briggs and Sykes had paid to Kempenfeldt Square. 'Do you think it's matter I can properly undertake, Geoffrey?' he asked bluntly.

'Yes, I do. I explained to Mr Prior our commitment to Jim Arnold's defence, but he feels in the circumstances that need not prohibit our acting.'

Maitland turned his eyes again on his new client, who was taking stock of him now as openly as he himself had done of the newcomer a moment ago. 'Someone in Kenyon Court is respons- ible for these extortion demands,' he said abruptly. 'And that raises a problem for me, because for Arnold's sake I want to find out who it is. Are you willing for me to try to do that?'

Prior had grimaced a little at his words, but he answered steadily enough. 'I think you're telling me that if you take my case you propose to do exactly what I was hoping you'd do; that is, investigate the matter thoroughly and try to prove who is really guilty.'

'You're right so far at any rate.'

'Rita told me that Joyce was the person to whom Henry gave the key to the cupboard where the money was deposited. I can quite see that places suspicion squarely on my shoulders, but I can only assure you –'

'Yes, you've already done so. You say you're quite prepared to deal with anything our enquiries may turn up?'

'Quite prepared. The only thing is,' – he looked from one of them to the other – 'the police seem to have got quite a good case against me.'

'Will you tell me about it?'

'I've already told Mr Horton.'

'Yes, so I suppose. Quite frankly, Mr Prior, it's his reaction to your story that encourages me to hear you out. But even now I can give you no guarantee that I'll do more than accept the brief he sends me and do the best I can in court.' He felt Geoffrey's eyes on him rather sardonically and turned his head to give him a half smile.

'That's understood,' said Prior. 'Where do you want me to begin?'

Maitland glanced at Horton. 'I think perhaps you'd better hear first about the party,' said Geoffrey.

'It wasn't exactly a party,' said Prior, 'more of a meeting really. A council of war perhaps.'

'How did it come about?'

'You'd been to see Rita Franklin in the afternoon, she told me all about that later, but at the time we met on Friday evening I hadn't heard any of the details. But it seems she talked to Henry when he came in, that you were undertaking this man Arnold's defence, and that for some reason you were interested in all the occupants of Kenyon Court. Henry – you don't know him, of course – is a little bit of an old maid and this worried him. So he rang each of us and asked us over for after-dinner drinks.'

'Wait a bit. Did he say why he was calling this meeting?'

'I don't know, Joyce took the call, she just said to me "We're invited to the Franklins", and it wasn't until we got there that I discovered what it was all about.'

'Since Mrs Franklin was only guessing at my interest in herself, her husband and their tenants, it's difficult to see what her husband told you.'

'Do you know, I think Henry expected one of us to get up on the spot and confess to some frightful crime which you were investigating. We'd all heard of you, of course, except Mamie who said she hadn't but I don't know whether that was true. Rita seemed to be a little uncomfortable at the storm she'd aroused, but when challenged she said there was no doubt you were an intelligent man and wouldn't have wasted her time if you hadn't had some reason to do so. Well we mulled the matter over for a time and various suggestions were made, but of course it wasn't until later, after the police enquiries got under way, that we heard about the protection money, so nothing that was said was very intelligent.'

'Do you think that Mrs Franklin's contribution to this discussion would have been sufficient to alert a person with something on his or her conscience?'

'Oh yes, she was quite definite you were after something, and knowing what we all did about you –'

'Yes, I see.' Maitland cut him off in mid-sentence rather unceremoniously. 'I suppose you know where all this supposition is tending, Mr Prior.'

'To the fact that someone in the house was the brains behind the extortion, and that Joyce was his accomplice. Therefore she was killed to keep her quiet, because, of course, once Henry had told the police that she had the key to that cupboard she would have been the first person they'd have talked to.'

'There's a further corollary too,' Antony pointed out.

'Yes I know, that I'm the most likely person to have been involved with her. I can only assure you –'

'Save that for later.' Maitland was unceremonious again. 'What you've told me so far isn't sufficient to worry you about the police's attitude. There must be more to it.'

'I was telling you about the meeting. We all know each other pretty well, and after we'd thrashed the subject out as well as we could – which, as I explained, wasn't very helpful really – we started talking about other things, and about eleven o'clock, just when I was thinking of suggesting that we should break up, Joyce sudeenly keeled over, out cold, and nothing we could do would rouse her. So Henry called our doctor while I carried her through to her own room; we're just across the hall, you know, from the Franklins' flat. When Henry followed me he said he'd called the ambulance as well, which was lucky as it turned out because the doctor immediately said she should be taken to hospital. He said she was in a deep coma, and of course started asking what she'd had to eat and drink, that sort of thing. I went along in the ambulance and hung around while they did whatever it is they do in these cases, and about two in the morning they told me she was dead.'

'When she first . . . keeled over was the phrase you used, wasn't it? When that happened, what was your first thought? Did you think she was drunk perhaps?'

'It wasn't by any means a teetotal evening,' said Prior, 'but she hadn't had anything beyond the usual. I knew she must be very ill, but I couldn't think of anything that would have affected her like that.'

'And after they told you –?'

'The doctor also told me he couldn't give a certificate. I knew that was natural enough when she hadn't been ill and hadn't seen him for ages, and of course I thought then that she'd died of natural causes. It wasn't until the police came round on Saturday that I found otherwise and then they made the connection with this protection business, and the whole thing seemed more puzzling than ever. And of course Joyce was the obvious person to have asked about that, only it was too late.'

'Did they tell you what the poison was and how long it had been taken before she collapsed?'

'Not exactly.'

'Now what do you mean by that, Mr Prior?'

'Only that they said there hadn't been time for all the tests that would have to be done, both to find out what had killed her, and the quantity used, and to give an estimate of how long it would have taken to work. Doctor Sutcliffe – that's our man – would only say that he thought one of the synthetic analgesics had been used, because they're less inclined than morphine for instance to cause vomiting before the coma ensues. I don't know if you know much about them, but death occurs with respiratory failure, following the coma which we all observed.'

'I don't know much about them, but you seem to.'

'Well yes, because . . . the police think they know exactly what she was given,' he concluded.

'Do they indeed? You're going to have to explain that, Mr Prior.'

'They think it was Methorphinian.'

'This is Chief Inspector Sykes you're talking about?'

'Yes and an Inspector Mayhew.'

'It isn't like Sykes to make wild guesses.'

'It wasn't exactly a guess. You see he found an almost empty bottle of the stuff in my bathroom cabinet. My mother died of cancer about five years ago, she was in a good deal of pain and that was what the doctor gave her because she hated injections and Methorphinian is well tolerated when given orally.'

'Why did you keep it?'

'I haven't the faintest idea. It was with the stuff the nursing home sent round after she died, and I suppose I put it away without thinking.'

'How much was left when the police found it?'

'Five tablets. They'd asked my permission to look round –'

'You might be sure Sykes would do everything by the book. But what interests me at the moment, Mr Prior, is whether that is the quantity the bottle held when you put it away five years ago.'

'I'm sorry, I can't tell you. I have the impression there were more tablets, but I could well be wrong about that.'

'Then let's see who else besides yourself would have had access to them.'

'Joyce herself, of course. Any one of our friends who has visited us in the last five years, and who may have used the bathroom while he was there.'

'And Mrs Prior? Could she have committed suicide?'

'I wondered about that, of course, but I think I discounted it for the same reason that the police gave for doing so. The natural thing in that case would have been to take the tablets when she went to bed, she'd probably be dead then before morning, whereas as it was I suppose there was a faint chance we might have saved her.'

'That's a possibility though.' Maitland was fumbling for one of his tattered envelopes on which to make a note. 'There are people who make the attempt at suicide and have no intention of really carrying it out, who rely on somebody stopping them while there's still time. That would be a point in court, wouldn't it, Geoffrey?'

'It certainly would, but we haven't got that far yet.'

'No, we haven't. If Sykes only thought of this – what did you call it? –'

'Methorphinian.'

'Well, if Sykes only thought of it when he visited you, he'd have to go away again and put it up to the doctors. It should then have been fairly easy to confirm or deny his thesis, even to make an estimate of the amount taken and how long it would need to produce the coma you've described. Have you seen Sykes and Mayhew again?'

'Yes, yesterday morning. It was telling Rita about that interview that made her advise me to consult you. They told me that they were indeed right about the drug, but that the doctors wouldn't commit themselves further than to say it had probably been administered between half-past seven and half-past nine on Friday evening.'

Maitland made another note. 'Is the stuff soluble?' he demanded.

'I know those particular tablets were, the ones my mother used to take, because she didn't like swallowing pills much more than she liked injections. The doctor was really very kind to her, made the things up so that they'd dissolve in a glass of water, and had a faintly lemony taste.'

'Ideal for adding to a drink then. I gather the party grew convivial after a while.'

'There were drinks on hand from the beginning.'

'What did Mrs Prior drink?'

'Her favourite was gin and tonic . . . with a slice of lemon.'

'What time did you meet in the Franklins' flat?'

'About half-past eight. We got straight up from the dinner-table, and didn't even clear the things away.'

'Had you had something to drink before that, after you got home for instance?'

'It was a case of Joyce getting home actually. I'm between jobs, and she doesn't get back from the shop – the one that used to be Henry Franklin's, you know – until about six o'clock. We had a glass of sherry, and some white wine with dinner. It's quite possible the stuff could have been dissolved in the wine, but not, I think, in anything as small as a sherry glass. I've no idea how much was used but it must have been a fair amount.'

'So it's possible she had taken the poison before you got to the Franklins'. Were the wine-glasses you used at dinner washed up?'

'Yes. I was restless when I got back from the hospital, knew I couldn't sleep, so I did the dinner dishes then.'

'I see. We must make a point to query the doctor's findings, there's usually a good deal of latitude in these matters.'

'I reminded you a few minutes ago, if we ever get to court,' said Geoffrey.

'Exactly. Now about the gathering in the Franklins' flat, Henry Franklin, I suppose, would be pouring the drinks?'

'The first round certainly. After that the duty of refills was shared out among the men, we always made a habit of that when we got together. I know I refilled Mamie's glass, and Charles's, but I think it was later in the evening.'

'You're telling me that if it was done at the party it must have been by one of the people who actually poured your wife a gin and tonic?'

'Yes, I think so. Except for refills we all stayed more or less in our places, it would have been awfully obvious for anyone to have gone to Joyce's side and added the stuff to her glass.'

'I suppose it would. But any of the four men might have had the opportunity?'

'Yes, I think so, but the four men, may I remind you, include me.'

'I'm well aware of it. So the next question to arise is, who of these people knew that you had the stuff in your bathroom cupboard?'

'Any one of them might have looked in I suppose, but unless they knew what Methorphinian was, why should they have thought of using it?'

'You never discussed your mother's illness with any of them?'

'No, that happened before we came to Kenyon Court. I'm surprised really that that bottle didn't get thrown out in the move, but there it was and to tell you the truth I don't blame the police for feeling suspicious.'

'Mrs Prior however must surely have known what it was.'

'I wish I could tell you we had a long chat about it only a week before, but I'm afraid it wouldn't be true. She went with me to visit mother sometimes, of course, and she must have seen me mix the tablets into a glass of water for her. But I can't recall that she took any interest in what they were, she used to say medical matters bored her.'

'I see. Why did your wife want to divorce you, Mr Prior?'

'It was I who wanted the divorce.'

'The question still stands.'

'I suppose we'd been growing apart from some time, our interests are so very different. But you know how it is, one gets used to things. I'd no real desire to make a change. Only then I discovered, quite by accident, that she'd been having an affair with some fellow. I suppose I shouldn't blame her too much, I was often away for quite long periods, but after that I didn't feel I wanted to go on.'

'You said she'd been seeing a solicitor?'

'Yes, I was quite willing to let her initiate the action. Meanwhile I was sleeping on the sofa in my den. The idea was that I'd be going abroad anyway in a month's time, by the time I came back to England it would be all over.'

'Have the police questioned you about this extortion business?'

'Certainly they have. That was on Sunday morning. There was nothing I could tell them, I knew nothing at all about it. I didn't even know Joyce had the key to the cupboard.'

'I think we must face the fact, however, that your being away so often would be one explanation of that last fact.'

'You mean that I couldn't have managed without her. That's true, of course.'

'How did you find out she'd been unfaithful to you?'

'An anonymous phone call, a woman's voice.'

'Not one that you recognised?'

'No, I'd never heard it before.'

'And you believed what the woman said, just like that?'

'No, of course not. But I told Joyce what had happened, and she admitted it quite readily. I can only think she was even more tired of me than I was of her.'

'It certainly complicates matters. This anonymous woman, did she give you any idea who the man might be?'

'No idea at all.'

'And you can't make a guess?' Prior shook his head. 'Did Mrs Prior say nothing when you spoke to her to give you any clue?'

'Nothing at all, except that their affection for each other was founded on similarity of interests. So now I'm wondering –'

'Yes?' prompted Maitland when Prior broke off.

'Whether perhaps it was the man behind this extortion racket, and the community of interests she mentioned was the money they were making.'

'Yes, that would seem to be a possibility. Well, Geoffrey, what do you make of all this?'

'Mr Prior tells me that so far as he knows that's the sum of the police's case. I think in the circumstances they're bound to connect Mrs Prior's death with the protection business, and I don't think they'll make a move against Mr Prior unless they can connect him definitely with that.'

'I'm inclined to agree with you. All the same, Mr Prior, I should keep Mr Horton's telephone number handy, and if any further questions arise just say you'd like to see him before you answer them.'

'And if I'm arrested?'

'Mr Horton and I will talk again.'

Prior was on his feet. 'Does that mean you don't believe a word I've been telling you?' he demanded.

'It means exactly what I said, no more, no less.'

'Well, I'll tell you one thing, I almost wish they would arrest me if that would make you take an interest in the matter. After all if it's let rest here, what are people going to think? They'll point me out for the rest of my life as the man who probably killed his wife, and I'd have no chance at all to defend myself.'

'Yes, I see your point. All the same, Mr Prior, I wouldn't be too keen on this arrest business. Things might not work out exactly as you hope.'

Sir Nicholas had already left chambers by the time Antony was free, and when he got back to his own quarters in Kempenfeldt Square it was to find that his uncle and Vera had invited them-selves to dinner. This didn't really surprise him, Sir Nicholas he knew would have been the guiding spirit in the move, and to Vera would fall the task of placating Mrs Stokes when the meal she had prepared went uneaten. What did surprise him, however, was that the subject of Jim Arnold and the protection racket, and Archibald Prior and the murder, was not brought up until they were sitting over their cognac. For himself he would have been content to let it lie even longer, but he was in no doubt about his uncle's deter-mination to get the whole story.

So he recounted without interruption the story that Archibald Prior had told him. 'Nowhere near a watertight case,' said Vera gruffly when he had finished.

'No, but even Prior admitted that he couldn't blame the police for being suspicious.'

'And what does Geoffrey think?' asked Sir Nicholas.

'I never had the chance to ask him except in Prior's presence. They left together. But I gather he agrees with Vera that as things stand at the moment they couldn't make it stick.'

'And what do you think, Antony?' Jenny put in.

'I think the points the police have against Prior are rather more serious, love. For instance, those tablets with the long, unpro-nounceable name. I can quite see him keeping them without any nefarious intention, but when he needed them there they were. That's what the police will say.'

'What do you think?' Jenny insisted.

'I think they were probably used to kill Mrs Prior, but anyone in the house had access to them. I'm inclined to believe Prior when he says *he* didn't use them.'

'I knew it!' said Sir Nicholas in a triumphant tone. 'Have you ever rummaged in someone else's bathroom cabinet, Antony?'

'Well . . . no.'

'I have,' said Jenny, 'but only if I was staying in the house, and I was told to look there for aspirin or something.'

'Got a point there, Antony,' said Vera. 'Even if they had a chance to see them how would they have known what they were?'

'I can't answer either of those things, Vera.'

'And to come to opportunity,' said Sir Nicholas inexorably, 'there's no doubt it would have been easier to introduce the stuff to the wine that that woman drank at dinner, rather than do it in full view of seven other people . . . seven if you include the victim that is.'

'I admit all that, Uncle Nick, but the fact remains that nothing was known about the enquiries I was making until the meeting took place.'

'No, but there's this matter of the proposed divorce. There was some ill-will between them –'

'She'd admitted adultery, but they weren't so much at odds they weren't prepared to live in the same flat until his next assignment.'

'As he was the injured party, that in itself might be taken as a suspicious circumstance. If anything comes of all this, Antony, what do you suppose the prosecution will rely on for motive, her unfaithfulness, or the fact that they were partners in this extortion?'

'Both, I should think. But I don't agree that Prior was the chap who employed Alf and Stan, Uncle Nick.'

'So what do you propose to do?'

'In the ordinary way, nothing at this stage. But Prior's anxiety gives me an excuse for talking to the other people . . . don't you think?'

'On Jim Arnold's account?'

'Yes, but if I could find the man in the background of the protection racket that would go a long way towards clearing Prior.'

'And if you find that Prior himself was involved after all?'

'I don't think I shall,' said Maitland with more confidence than he felt. And then added more honestly, 'I'm not sure, Uncle Nick, how can I be? But I think it's worth a try.'

'Occurred to you, of course, that this man you're looking for is a pretty dangerous character,' said Vera. 'If what Chief Inspector Sykes told you is true, he's responsible for two deaths already, besides, presumably, Mrs Prior's murder, even though he didn't commit the first two himself.'

Antony glanced at Jenny. 'Whoever he is, any tendency to violence is obviously kept well under the surface,' he said. 'It doesn't take much in the way of guts to poison somebody, but that's rather a different matter from attempting assault and battery on a respectable lawyer in one's own home.'

'Is that supposed to comfort us?' asked Sir Nicholas of the room at large. 'I agree with you, Antony,' – and his eyes too went to Jenny's face – 'he isn't likely to prove violent during the interview. All the same you're going to find yourself right in the middle of a police investigation, which isn't going to make you popular with them. Frankly it's Briggs I'm concerned about, not your physical safety.'

'So am I,' said Vera.

'But I can't let this opportunity slip by, and I think you're making a mountain out of a mole-hill, both of you,' said Antony. 'The worst that can happen is that Sykes will accuse me again of not being completely open with him, which he doesn't expect me to be any-way, and if I do get the information we both want he won't be able to go on saying that for very long because I shall bring it out with all the publicity I can manage during Jim Arnold's trial.'

'You're not going to try that trick of calling Chief Superintendent Briggs again?' said Sir Nicholas.

'No, it would be the detective in charge of the investigation into the extortion this time, but that ought to suffice. Don't you see, Uncle Nick, if I could get an admission from him that they had had to give way to an investigation of murder that was believed to have been done by the man responsible for Jim being victimised . . . it would open a whole new vista, I could call anyone from Kenyon Court that I liked.'

'Unorthodox,' said Sir Nicholas, as briefly as Vera herself might have done.

'Yes, I dare say, but I may as well live up to my reputation after all. Besides, sir, what would *you* do?'

At that his uncle smiled. 'Exactly the same thing,' he admitted. 'But I should also pray in the meantime that this man Alf Gray will agree to identify the person who accosted him in a pub one evening.'

'That would be the easy way out, certainly,' said Antony, 'but

118

having seen the gentleman myself I'm not too optimistic.' And before he could say anything else the telephone rang, and he got up with a murmured apology to cross the room and answer it.

'I thought I'd better let you know,' said Geoffrey, without wasting time on a greeting, 'that Archibald Prior has been arrested for the murder of his wife. Can you take the magistrate's court hearing tomorrow?'

'Not a hope. Would you like me to send Derek?'

'Yes, I think that would be the best thing. Not that there'll be anything to do, really, I suppose we'll reserve our defence ... or am I anticipating matters by assuming you'll take the case?'

'No, I've already made up my mind to do so.'

'I thought you had,' said Geoffrey with a certain amount of satisfaction in his tone. 'Will you be in court all day?'

'Pretty well, I think. Could you stay at the office until I get back to chambers? I'll ring you then and find out what other titbits the prosecution has for our undoing.'

'Yes, I'll do that. Antony, are you going to – to –'

'To meddle?' said Antony. 'Uncle Nick tells me I shouldn't, Vera tells me I shouldn't, and I've no doubt you're going to add your voice to the chorus at any moment. But I think it's too good an opportunity to miss and in a way it's a good thing this has happened –'

'I don't suppose Prior agrees with you.'

'No, I've no doubt he doesn't, but what I was going to say was that it gives us the best of excuses for seeing the rest of the people in the house.'

'I suppose that's true,' said Geoffrey without enthusiasm. 'Do you want appointments made? When are you going to be free?'

'With any luck my present client will be tucked up safely in jail by Thursday night,' said Antony callously, 'but if I don't spend some time on Friday with my other workload I'll be in a hell of a mess next week. In any case – if you don't mind, of course – it might be most convenient to catch the Kenyon Court lot at the weekend. The Franklins, of course, are retired, but the others might not find it so easy to be free.'

'I don't mind,' said Geoffrey, but still without enthusiasm. 'I'll try to set up something for Saturday then.'

'Good. I suppose there's no chance of Jim Arnold's case coming on too soon.'

'I heard today. Possibly in about a fortnight's time. Can you be ready?'

'That's on the knees of the gods. Give me a call during the week, there's a good chap, and I shall see you, I hope, some time on Saturday.'

He got back to the fireside to find that Jenny had replenished the glasses while he was gone. 'I gather,' said Sir Nicholas, 'that your client has been arrested and that you now consider yourself to have the best of reasons for asking indiscriminate questions. I can only say, to borrow a colloquialism from your aunt, watch your step.'

'I shall be discretion itself,' Antony promised; he was beginning to get used to these occasional lapses on his uncle's part. But it cannot be said that any of his hearers – even Jenny – placed much reliance on the assurance.

When Maitland got back to chambers the next evening it was to learn that Derek Stringer had already left. He put through his call to Geoffrey straight away, therefore, and was greeted by the rather grumpy statement, 'Committed for trial, of course. What did you expect?'

'It's certainly no surprise,' Maitland acknowledged. 'Did the police put on all their evidence?'

'So far as I know, though of course I've got no papers yet. The trouble is, Antony, they've got one more point that seems to put rather a different complexion on things.'

'The worst complexion?' Maitland asked.

'Well, to my mind . . . but I'd better tell you. They got an order to examine Joyce Prior's bank accounts, to go into her affairs in general. She'd made regular deposits in cash, totalling about ten thousand pounds a month. Not that it stayed on deposit, she had all sorts of holdings, well diversified. So then they asked our client for permission to go into his affairs too, and apparently he gave it quite readily. This was before he got in touch with me. He told them his account, unlike his wife's is with Bramley's Bank, and everything was quite in order, salary cheques, drawings for expenses, household expenses too, of course, nothing out of the way. He wasn't so adventurous as his wife, or perhaps he had less time to spend on his financial affairs. His investing consisted of fairly regular transfers to his deposit account.'

'That all sounds quite reasonable. What are you moaning about?'

'You'll see in a minute. It was then that the manager of the branch where Mrs Prior banked suddenly came up with the infor-mation that Archibald Prior had had a deposit account there too, into which regular deposits of five thousand pounds in cash had been made by his wife. Naturally, I saw him as soon as the hearing was over and asked for an explanation. The only thing he could think of to say was that he knew nothing at all about the account.'

'Had it been opened by him?'

'Apparently. One of those cards the banks use for specimen signatures was produced, and they called a witness to testify that it was the accused's handwriting but even I could see that it must be.'

'Did you ask him whether his wife ever gave him things for signature? She might have opened the two accounts at the same time and brought the card back for him –'

'He said she dealt with all their business affairs, and sometimes he signed cheques and other things just because she put them in front of him. I thought it was rather weak myself.'

'No, Rita Franklin said he was rather vague about things like that. How long had all this been going on?'

'Just about the five years Jim Arnold says the extortion had been taking place.'

'And no withdrawals had been made in the meantime? It must be a pretty sizeable fund by now.' Antony took out an envelope and began to do sums on the back of it.

'It is,' said Geoffrey grimly.

'Yes, but look here.' Maitland was staring at the results of his calculations. 'Fifteen thousand a month between them, that's nowhere near enough.'

'I'd have thought it was pretty good going myself.'

'That's not what I meant. Stan Bond said they worked a five-day week, and Don Tudor told me he was paying two hundred pounds a month. Supposing Stan and Alf made ten calls a day –'

'Yes, I see what you mean. But it won't do, Antony, there's nothing to have stopped Prior having a dozen such accounts round the town.'

'No, I suppose not. You say he denied all knowledge of this one?'

'He did. But you must see it's a strong point for the prosecution, I mean, if he isn't the man concerned why should he be getting anything at all?'

'Insurance, perhaps.'

'But a sum like that?' Geoffrey sounded shocked. Then when Antony didn't reply immediately he went on, 'Do you still want me to make those appointments?'

'Oh yes, I think so, don't you?'

'You've made up your mind,' said Geoffrey accusingly.

'I only wish I had. Still, I'd like to give Jim Arnold a chance, and after all we've no right to set ourselves up as judges of Archibald Prior's guilt or innocence.'

'No right at all,' Geoffrey conceded, 'but –'

'Don't tell me. Joan doesn't like you working weekends,' said Antony. 'Well, Jenny doesn't either, but she's willing to stretch a point when it's in a good cause.'

But he was thoughtful as he went home a little while later. Sir Nicholas and Vera were with Jenny when he arrived, but this was no more than he expected on a Tuesday evening. He gave them the news immediately, to get it over with, and listened more meekly than usual to his uncle's strictures on his proposed course of conduct.

I

By the time Saturday came round, which was the first opportunity Maitland had had for turning his attention to Archibald Prior's affairs, Geoffrey Horton arrived at Kempenfeldt Square in time for breakfast with a good deal more information for him concerning the Crown's case. 'You don't want to hear about the police or medical evidence,' he stated definitely. 'In any case it's all there in what you've got if you care to read it.' He knew well enough that this wouldn't be until the court hearing was imminent, when Antony would turn his unwilling attention to his brief.

'Wait a bit. There's one part of the police evidence I'm interested in.'

'I should have remembered that. Yes, they're calling for evidence about the protection racket, they evidently decided that's the best peg to hang motive on.'

'I thought they would. What next Geoffrey?'

'Oh, evidence from the bank about both the accounts that the Priors held. They don't seem to have been able to find any others, by the way, but that isn't to say they're non-existent. Then they're calling both your friends, Stan and Alf. Stan is still singing like a canary, as I'm sure Sir Nicholas would hate to hear me say; but Alf has refused to answer all questions so far, and I don't think anybody hopes he'll change his mind and identify his principal in court.'

'He may not be there. The principal, I mean.'

'You know I thought at first that Prior was innocent,' said Geoffrey, 'but this money business –'

'It's absolutely inconclusive,' said Maitland definitely. 'However, you'd got as far as Alf and Stan.'

'Yes, then the two Franklins. He, of course, is to confirm that Joyce Prior had the key to the cupboard in question, and I think

124

her part is mainly to give evidence as to the relationship between their neighbours. It seems Mrs Prior confided in her to a certain extent. After all, she was left alone for quite long periods.'

'That's all very well, but did she tell Rita Franklin who the man was?'

'Not according to Mrs Franklin's proof. Joyce hinted there was somebody but that was all, and said that she felt Archie was neglecting her and was sick and tired of it.'

'What about the first floor tenants?'

'They aren't being called at all.'

'Have the Franklins been questioned about the party . . . the gathering . . . the meeting . . . whatever you like to call it?'

'Yes, but mainly as to Joyce Prior's deportment, and her husband's reaction when she collapsed. Apart from that the police don't seem to regard it as important.'

'Well, we can remedy that,' said Maitland with an air of determination.

'If you mean by calling the Dickinsons and the Shelleys, what could you ask them that would be helpful?'

'Just what I asked our client: who had the opportunity of mixing Mrs Prior a lethal gin and tonic?'

'According to him all the men had the opportunity, but that's not to say that one of them did.'

'Had those glasses been washed up too?'

'They had. Not unreasonably, I think.'

'No, of course not, but the police are obviously relying heavily on the fact that Prior could have given her the drug when they had dinner. We can't just leave it at that.'

'No, and that means,' said Geoffrey, not without malice, 'that you're going to have to go into the medical evidence pretty thoroughly in order to shake their expert as to the time that would have elapsed between the drug being given and her passing out.'

'So it does. Oh hell,' said Maitland, not without emotion. 'I suppose you've got hold of someone too, to put our side of the case?'

'It's all in that rather modest pile of documents on your desk,' Geoffrey pointed out. 'On their side there's also, of course, the doctor who attended old Mrs Prior in her last illness. He can give the date when the last prescription was dispensed, which the date when the last prescription was dispensed, which apparently was only a day or two before she died. That looks very much as though there were considerably more than five in the bottle when the old lady died, leading inescapably to the conclusion that they were the agents of Joyce Prior's death.'

'I always thought they were.'

'Which raises a number of difficulties. Prior knew what Methorphinian was, and its properties.'

'So did his wife presumably.'

'Yes, but I think Sykes's objection holds. If she was set on self-destruction – and we have no evidence to that effect – she'd have done it in bed in comfort. That seems to be the almost invariable choice of all suicides.'

'You're right, of course.'

'And as you pointed out yourself, even though there's a lot of visiting between the various tenants, who would have known the stuff was there? And if they had known by chance, would they have known its properties?'

'I may have said that, or you may have pointed it out to me in your role of candid friend,' said Antony gloomily. 'I'd like to have talked to Henry Franklin though. Do you realise that, after our client, whom I admit has the best claim to the role, he's the most likely murderer?'

'How do you make that out?'

'I don't know how long Joyce Prior worked for him, but I do gather it was a number of years, and she'd been taken on now as manager of the shop he sold when he retired. We may even find that's the reason the Priors went to live in Kenyon Court, because of their association.'

'Are you hinting that he might have been the mysterious lover?'

'It's possible, but by no means certain. No, all I'm saying is that if he were the man behind the extortion, Joyce would have been a very likely candidate as his accomplice. Rita seems to have rather an open nature, besides being a very intelligent woman. Anyway, for all I know she may be too honest to indulge in a caper like that.'

'Well, I can't offer you the opportunity of talking to Henry Franklin immediately,' said Geoffrey, 'but he will be called by the prosecution when Jim Arnold comes to trial, and that won't be very long now.'

'How long?'

'A little earlier than we anticipated. Tuesday or Wednesday of next week I should think.'

'I see. A delicate situation, Geoffrey, or hadn't you thought of that?'

'Of course I'd thought of it. But you'll be entitled to question Franklin about everything but the actual murder. After all the fact that he was the victim of a protection racket is very much a part of our case on Jim's behalf.'

'So it is,' said Antony, cheering. He passed his cup to Jenny for a refill. 'And if we talk to the others today . . . how did they sound when you phoned them, Geoffrey?'

'Stuffy in the case of Mr Dickinson, who happened to answer the phone –'

'He's a civil servant,' Antony reminded Jenny.

'– and quite friendly but definitely upset in the case of Mrs Shelley. I made an appointment with the Dickinsons for ten-thirty, and said we'd see the Shelleys immediately after we've talked to them, because I didn't know quite how long it would take. It's no good taking two bites at a cherry.'

'Certainly not. And as you have the car here . . . I suppose we'd better leave before long, and could you fix something that won't spoil for lunch, Jenny? Then it won't matter if we're a bit li te.'

Jenny, who was only too used to late meals or even skipped ones, agreed without any surprise to his request. 'But I think Vera's free this morning,' she said very seriously. 'It would be good practice for her, are you ture you wouldn't like her to drive you?'

'Not on your life,' said Antony, with every appearance of alarm. 'It was bad enough when she felt herself still a learner, but now that she's full of self-confidence, it's a case of *sauve qui peut.*'

'Coward,' said Jenny without animosity. 'Who had to drive all over London with her while she was learning? If I could do that, you ought to be able to put up with her for an hour or so.'

'We wouldn't dream of keeping her waiting,' said Antony firmly. 'Geoffrey'd be a nervous wreck thinking of her sitting in the car outside.' He broke off when he saw Jenny smiling. 'I don't believe for an instant she suggested driving us, love. For one thing, how could she know –?'

'She's quite as capable as I am of drawing her own conclusions,' said Jenny. 'However, If you're both back for lunch I may forgive you, Geoffrey, for taking Antony out at the weekend.' And as Geoffrey began to protest that if anyone was responsible for this over-time it was Maitland, she got up with an air of decision and began to clear the table around them.

II

As Rufus Dickinson had promised in his brief conversation with Geoffrey over the telephone, both he and his wife were at home when Maitland and Horton arrived only a little late for their appointment. They made their way up to the first floor without seeing anybody, and found that the Dickinsons' flat was, as might have been expected, directly over the one occupied by the Priors. The woman who opened the door to them was tall and dark and had an air of chic about her not usually observed except in the more exclusive West End hotels. 'Doctor Dickinson?' Geoffrey enquired tentatively, at which she nodded and replied, also with a question in her voice, 'Mr Horton?' After that she stood back and let them into the tiny hall, for the moment eyeing Antony appraisingly. 'You must be the Mr Maitland of whom everybody says I should have heard,' she remarked challengingly. 'Well, I never did.'

'That's good,' said Antony before his companion could speak. 'The newspapers print an awful lot of nonsense, don't they? It's much better to start from scratch.'

She made no direct reply to that, only eyed him a moment or two longer and then turned on her heel and led the way into the living-room. A rather soulless room, Antony thought it, and definitely over-tidy, though there were two desks whose closed lids might have concealed any amount of litter. 'Mr Horton and Mr Maitland,' said Mamie Dickinson casually. 'My husband, Rufus.'

A murmured greeting followed this rather off-hand introduction. Rufus Dickinson had been sitting by the window, but now he got up and came back to the group of chairs around the hearth. 'Not quite cold enough for a fire, is it?' he asked. 'But sit down,

128

won't you, and tell us what this is all about? We're both rather curious.'

If as an infant he'd had a feathering of sandy hair which had led his parents to expect him to grow up a redhead, this had long since given way to a dark, straight thatch, only scantily streaked with grey. It seemed as though it were the custom in this building for there to be a fair age disparity between husband and wife, and the Dickinsons were no exception; there must have been fifteen years between them.

'There are a few questions –' Geoffrey began.

'Yes, I'm sure there are.' They were seated by now but in a moment Mamie Dickinson was on her feet again, offering cigarettes. 'You're thinking of Archie Prior, I suppose,' Rufus went on, 'but I don't think that's a matter that either my wife or I wish to get mixed up in.'

'I can quite understand that,' said Geoffrey, 'but –'

'The trouble is, you see,' Maitland interrupted him, 'you are mixed up in it, willy nilly.'

'Why? Because we happened to be there when poor Joyce collapsed?'

'That and other things.'

'Such as what?'

'You know why Mr Franklin called all his tenants together that night?'

'Because of some nonsense of Rita's, she seemed to have got it into her head that you suspect one of us of something . . . it was all very vague . . . and Henry, being a bit of a fusspot, wanted to talk it over.'

'And what was the result of your deliberations?'

'Nothing at all, as you can imagine. We never even reached a definite conclusion as to what it was all about.'

'Someone knew,' said Antony flatly. 'For instance, what was Mrs Prior's reaction while this conversation was going on?'

'She seemed as bewildered as any of us,' said Doctor Dickinson. 'I'm not quite sure myself even now, but I gather from what Henry says that one of us is suspected of being a criminal, and that it has something to do with the man who burgled his apartment.'

'That's near enough,' said Antony, smiling at her. 'But at the time you were all completely in the dark?'

'Completely.'

'Including Mr Prior?'

'Yes, certainly. He was just as puzzled as anybody.'

'Would you be willing to give evidence to that effect, Doctor Dickinson?'

'I really think that would be most inappropriate,' interrupted Dickinson, and for the first time Antony heard the note of stuffiness that Geoffrey had mentioned in his voice. He also thought he heard something else: a protectiveness that he was sure the woman would resent. An ill-assorted couple, but Rufus at least seemed to be devoted to his wife. 'Mamie's professional standing –'

'Would certainly not be harmed by swearing to something she believes to be true,' said Maitland gently. 'What was your impression, Mr Dickinson?'

'I dare say I'm not a very observant man. I saw nothing out of the ordinary in anybody's manner.'

'I see. Thank you. Now when you arrived at the Franklins' that evening . . . will you tell me exactly what happened?'

'What was said you mean? Henry seemed disturbed –'

'No, I meant where you all sat, who poured the drinks, things like that.'

'Oh, I see. Well, we all arrived more or less together, which wasn't surprising since we all live so near. Henry asked each of us our preference as to drinks, though he must have known it perfectly well already, and provided us according to our requests.'

'Mrs Prior was drinking gin and tonic?'

'Yes, she always did. But I don't like this at all, Mr Maitland.' Dickinson's tone had sharpened. 'Are you trying to imply that the poison, the drug, whatever it was, was given to her during the time we were all together?'

'I'm not implying anything, I'm seeking information, that's all.'

'I don't think we can help you. Henry knew the name of the drug too, which I've forgotten, but I understand it is sometimes used for medicinal purposes, so how could a sufficient quantity have been put into her glass without anybody noticing?'

'It might have been done when the drinks were mixed,' said Mamie positively.

130

'Oh you think so, do you? I suppose you also remember that if refills were needed it was the men who provided them.'

'Four men, four rounds?' said Maitland thoughtfully.

'Nothing of the sort. I don't suppose anyone had more than one or two drinks, unless it was you, my dear,' he added looking at Doctor Dickinson with a smile that was pure malice. Antony began to think that perhaps his first impression had been a mistaken one.

'I dare say I did, what of it?' She remained completely unruffled. 'I believe Archie provided me with my second and Charles with my third, if the information is of any interest to you. And I was drinking scotch on the rocks. But you're quite right, Mr Maitland, it could only have been done when the drink was actually poured. These are fair-sized rooms you know, nobody was sitting particularly close to anybody else, and though as far as I remember Charles and Joyce shared a table for their glasses, he couldn't possibly have added anything to hers without somebody knowing.'

'That's Charles Shelley, your neighbour across the hall on this floor?'

'Yes. As you must have heard, he and Alfreda were there too. Which was silly really because nobody – even me – could think for a moment that either of them was mixed up in anything shady.'

'Why do you except yourself, Doctor Dickinson, or rather put yourself in a different category from the rest of the people who live here?'

'Because I'm the odd man out, the odd woman out –'

'Odd person,' said Rufus rather sneeringly.

'Yes, if you prefer it. I believe in the women's movement –'

'Even to the extent of feeling that they should be suspected equally with the men of having poisoned Joyce,' said Rufus, still sarcastically.

'Yes, if the facts weren't against it. I also don't believe in your socialised medicine, Mr Maitland, and practise outside the National Health Service. Even my husband, who is what I believe you call a true blue Tory, disapproves of my attitude there.'

'I only think, my dear,' said Rufus, more conciliatory now, so that Maitland became confused again, 'that it's a shame that your very able services should only be available to people who can pay for them.'

'Nonsense,' said Mamie. 'There are plenty of people ready to look after the others and feel noble doing it. The AMA –'

'Now don't let's get on to the American Medical Association,' said Rufus hurriedly. 'It's all very well you two coming here asking us all these questions, but why can't you accept the obvious? Archie poisoned her before ever they came across to the Franklins' flat.'

'Because I don't think that's what happened.'

'Well, he had as much opportunity as anybody else to do it after they got there.'

'No doubt. Do either of you remember if Mrs Prior asked for a refill?'

'I think she did,' said Mamie hesitantly.

'I just don't remember,' said her husband. 'In any case, if she did, I don't remember who gave it to her. Do you, my dear?'

Mamie Dickinson was frowning. 'No I don't,' she said. 'Though now I come to think about it I'm under the impression that she drank her first gin and tonic rather quickly, which was unusual for her. I don't think she asked for another, but I'm quite sure someone refilled her glass, perhaps when he saw it was empty.'

'And you can't remember who it was?'

'No, I'm afraid I can't. You must understand we were quite in the habit of getting together, there was very little formality about our meetings. Whoever was host would be only too grateful if someone else helped him out.'

'Now, that I find really interesting. Have you formed any professional opinion, Doctor Dickinson, as to how long the drug would have taken to work?'

'I'm sorry, no. It was one of the morphine derivatives, and the time it took to work would depend on a number of things. How much was given, of course, that's first on the list. Then, how long before or after she'd eaten, things like that. The pathologist would be able to tell you.'

'The trouble is he'll have formed some hard and fast opinions from which there'll be no shaking him,' said Maitland ruefully. 'And what can you tell me about the relationship between Archibald and Joyce Prior?'

To his surprise she flushed up at that, a thing he hadn't thought

132

possible, and then looked at her husband, waiting for him to answer. 'They were getting a divorce,' said Rufus. 'Not that I knew that on the evening in question, Henry told me since. And they seem to have been going about it in a reasonably civilised way. Archie would have been going away before very long and just wouldn't come back here. Meanwhile she was initiating the action.'

'And you know nothing of the reasons for this?' Antony insisted.

'Nothing at all. We've seen a good deal of them, though of course Archie is very often away from home. But I can't say we've ever been intimate.'

'Well, there's just one more question and then we'll leave you in peace. What time do you both get home in the afternoon on week-days?'

Rufus Dickinson frowned. 'That's an odd question,' he said.

'The reason for it will emerge in a moment,' Antony assured him.

'Well, the answer's simple from my point of view. I get in about five-thirty, within a few minutes either way.'

'And you, Doctor Dickinson?'

'I keep office hours theoretically, but you can never guarantee how much of your time an individual patient will take. Any time from five-thirty onwards, and I don't think I'm often after seven.'

'Well, the next question is, have either of you ever seen the two men there's been so much talk about coming into Kenyon Court between seven and eight o'clock, probably nearer eight?'

'We're usually having dinner by half-past seven, unless it's one of the evenings I'm extra late,' said Mamie. 'Have you seen them, Rufus?'

'No, I haven't. Are these the two men who were supposed to have used the cupboard in the hall to which Henry had given Joyce the key? He said the police were asking about it.'

'Yes those are the two.'

'Well I don't know what they were like –'

'Rough looking types, a tall one and a short one.'

'Then I certainly haven't seen them. And if they only came as far as the downstairs hall it's very unlikely that either of us should have done so. If we were having visitors, for instance, and went to the door to let them in, these two men wouldn't be upstairs.'

'No, that seems unlikely. The other question is, did you ever see Mrs Prior go to that cupboard?'

'I hardly noticed the thing, hardly knew there was a cupboard there until Henry mentioned it the other day. If I had seen Joyce, I can't say I'd have thought anything of it, but I'm pretty sure I never did. There is one thing though.'

'What is that?'

'I don't want to seem unco-operative, but it can't have any significance. Sometimes Joyce and I would leave about the same time in the morning, and she'd have an attaché case with her. I never thought it anything but quite natural.'

'What colour was it?'

'Black.'

'Thank you. Doctor Dickinson?'

'I think I may have seen the two men, several times, in fact. But it's hard to be sure, just from a description, and I didn't connect them with the cupboard.' She paused, and then continued with a question of her own, 'Are the police suggesting that Archie was Joyce's confederate, and that he killed her because he couldn't trust her now they were going to be divorced?'

'We shan't know exactly what the prosecution suggests until we get into court,' said Maitland inaccurately. 'But something like that seems to be the idea.'

'That would mean' – she was thinking it out – 'that someone controlled these two men's activities. Why couldn't it have been a woman . . . Joyce herself perhaps?'

'Theoretically no reason at all. Mrs Prior herself or Mrs Prior in partnership with another woman. I think the other person was a man though.'

'Because you don't think a woman would have been capable?' she flashed at him.

'Nothing of the sort. Forgive me, Doctor Dickinson, I really have a reason.'

'All right.' She smiled rather ruefully. 'And I'm afraid Rufus won't agree with me. But if there's anything I can say that will help Archie Prior in court, I'd be glad to be a witness. I don't see him as a criminal type, certainly not as a murderer.'

They left the Dickinsons arguing over that when they left a few minutes later. 'He's caught a tartar,' said Geoffrey as soon as he was sure the door had closed behind him.

'Do you think so? I rather liked her,' said Antony, 'and so, unless I'm very much mistaken, does he.' He glanced at his watch. 'Don't stand there arguing, there's a good chap,' he urged. 'Let's see what the Shelleys have to say for themselves.'

III

Charles and Alfreda Shelley had waited in for them as they had promised. They came to their front door together, as though they couldn't bear even this small separation, and they might, Maitland considered, have been deliberately made up to illustrate a picture entitled "We've been together now for forty years." They were much of a height, neither tall nor short, neither fat nor thin, and their hair was the same iron grey and in both cases naturally wavy. It was only when they were back in the living-room, with the morning light pouring in on them, that Antony realised that Mrs Shelley was a good deal the older of the two, and that Charles Shelley was probably younger than he looked at first glance. They were made to feel welcome, offered coffee and sweet biscuits, and when they finally settled down there was definitely a cosy air over the proceedings.

It was Alfreda who took the lead. 'We're so glad you came,' she said, 'because we can neither of us believe that Archie would do such a terrible thing.'

'What do you think happened then?'

'I'm afraid, I'm very much afraid Joyce must have done it herself. You see Archie was divorcing her.'

'I understood —'

'Yes, you're quite right,' Charles Shelley put in. 'She was initiating the proceedings, or whatever the correct way of putting it is, but Archie was actually the injured party.'

'He consulted Charles when he found out what was happening,' said Alfreda. 'You know how men will talk to one another, and he was really worried. He said —'

135

'Just a moment, my dear. I'm sure Mr Maitland and Mr Horton would rather hear this at first hand.' He turned back to them. 'Archie came to me and said he'd had an anonymous telephone call, a woman's voice telling him that when he was away Joyce was having an affair with another man. He wanted to know whether he should ignore the call or do something about it. I think he even had an idea of putting a private detective on to looking into the matter. I told him I didn't think that was a good idea, but that it was only fair that he should tell Joyce what had been said.'

'What happened then?'

'He – he confronted her,' said Charles, 'and she admitted the whole thing right away. She was a very attractive woman, you know.'

'Did she tell him the man's name?'

'No, that was one thing she was adamant about. I think from what Archie told me that she was much less upset about the whole thing than he was. He ... well he's much my age, or a little younger perhaps, but still old fashioned in these things. After we'd talked it over for a while he decided he wouldn't do anything to embarrass her, that's why he stayed in the flat until he was due to go away the next time, but he couldn't bear that the marriage should continue under the circumstances. I didn't think, I really didn't, that she was upset enough to kill herself, but it seems the only solution. Besides there was this other business of the money that was collected and brought here. If she'd found out about your enquiries –'

'She hadn't. I'd only seen Mrs Franklin, and I understand nothing was passed on to the tenants until you were all actually gathered in their flat.'

'I do think, if I'd had a guilty conscience, that Henry's rather odd summons might have alerted me,' said Charles Shelley. 'If that happened –'

'Yes, I see what you mean. Mr Horton and I, of course, have considered the possibility of suicide on Mrs Prior's part, and its value as a defence. If we were to call you two as witnesses –'

'We should certainly have no objection to saying what we think,' said Alfreda firmly. 'Should we, Charles?'

'No, my dear, certainly not. I can't think, though, that our testimony would be of very much use.'

'Perhaps not, but we have to try everything. Mr Shelley, you say Mr Prior had no idea who the other man might have been, but in your own mind did you make any guesses on that subject?'

'I think I might have wondered if perhaps somebody here in the building had been involved, we're all pretty close friends you see, and when Archie was away were inclined to try to stop Joyce feeling lonely. But Archie was quite firm that he had never heard the woman's voice before, so I don't think that could be true. An outsider couldn't have known.'

'No, I see. Let's pretend for a moment, however, that Mr Prior is innocent, and that Mrs Prior didn't kill herself. Where does that leave us?'

'Before she came home from the shop –' Alfreda hazarded.

'When I get into court I'm quite prepared to argue about the medical evidence until the cows come home,' said Maitland, smiling, 'but privately I'll admit I don't think the doctors could be so far out in their reckoning as that. The drug must have been given at dinner-time at the earliest and we're assuming Mr Prior's innocence for the moment . . . remember?'

'That brings us to the party. Oh dear, are you trying to tell me that we're all of us under suspicion?'

'Something like that,' said Antony cheerfully, and smiled at them again to take the sting out of the words.

'Well well, we must still try to help, I suppose. We weren't standing around, you know, but sitting discussing what you had said to Rita Franklin. Henry poured the first round of drinks, which was natural, after that the men helped themselves, and if one of us noticed that any of the women's glasses were empty we'd look after them too.'

'Who was sitting near Mrs Prior?'

'Charles on one side and Mamie Dickinson on the other,' said Alfreda promptly. 'And – you remember Charles, I remarked on this to you – Joyce usually used to sit sipping her drink for a couple of hours, but that evening she drank the first one rather quickly.'

'And do you remember who refilled her glass?'

She frowned over that. 'No, I'm afraid I don't. Do you Charles?'

'I'm afraid not.' I think all of us men were up one time or

another – I know I refilled my own glass – but I don't think I poured anybody a gin and tonic.'

'We'll have to leave it there then, but if you should remember –'

'Joyce killed herself,' said Alfreda firmly. 'Will you have some more coffee, Mr Maitland?'

'Thank you.' His empty cup changed hands, and was returned a moment later filled to the brim. 'I wonder how much you understand about the case that first brought me here to see Rita Franklin.'

'Not a great deal,' said Charles. 'Only what Henry has been able to tell me. But I gather some men had been extorting money from shopkeepers for what they call protection – frankly I didn't know this kind of thing went on in England – and the money was deposited here in the hall cupboard to which only Joyce had the key.'

'Extra keys can easily be made,' said Maitland.

'You mean that she may have had an accomplice and the accomplice killed her?'

'Something like that. The prosecution at Prior's trial will say, of course, that he's the most likely person to have been associated with her, and that because of the divorce he could no longer trust her.'

'But you don't believe that?'

'No, I don't,' said Maitland with as much emphasis as his doubts would allow him to infuse into his tone. 'Don't you think it much more likely that this liaison she was conducting was with her partner in crime?'

'I suppose it's possible.'

'Perhaps he too had come to have doubts of her. Perhaps he didn't like her telling Prior of his existence, even though she didn't name him. Perhaps the Priors' divorce was intended to force his hand in some way. There are a dozen possibilities.'

'You're saying the extortion is behind the whole thing, the motive for Joyce's death?'

'Yes, I think so. Anything else would be too much of a coincidence.'

'But that would mean . . . that would definitely mean one of us at the party.'

'I'm afraid so, but the matter is very far from proof yet. What I want to ask you now concerns my first client, Jim Arnold, a small shopkeeper in Fulham.'

'The man who was caught robbing Henry Franklin?'

'That's right. He's an old lag, which will go against him, but he's been going straight for the last seven or eight years, and as he only went back to crime because he was being bled white by this protection racket I have a good deal of sympathy for him.'

'Poor man,' said Alfreda Shelley. He got the impression that though she meant what she said she didn't understand at all.

'Well, it's a long story and I won't go into it now, but I want to put on the best defence I can for him. And in this case it can only be that there were extenuating circumstances. I can certainly get a description of Joyce Prior's involvement and subsequent death introduced and I hope the judge will allow some discussion of the party too. If he does will you give evidence? Just as you've done now, about your fairly frequent meetings and lack of formality with each other.'

'I don't see how it can help,' said Charles slowly, 'but we'll certainly do so if you think it can do any good.'

'Yes, of course,' said Alfreda, but now she sounded bewildered. ('As well she might,' said Geoffrey later, when they had left Kenyon Court.)

But the next question, asked when Maitland had abandoned hope of getting anything useful, received a more helpful reply. One evening about two years ago, when they had had an early dinner and were going out to the cinema, they had encountered two men in the entrance who could only have been Alf and Stan. Afreda had asked, 'I wonder who those two men could have been?' as soon as they were out of earshot, and Charles had said reassuringly, 'Workmen of some kind, I suppose.' And as they had heard Henry Franklin's door open just as they were leaving the building they were pretty sure that must have been the case.

IV

Maitland and Horton got back to Kempenfeldt Square to find that

139

Antony's careful apologies for cancelling the usual arrangement with Sir Nicholas and Vera had been ignored. Mrs Stokes would be only too happy to hold luncheon until Mr Maitland and Mr Horton returned. Gibbs relayed the information sourly, and Antony exchanged a grin with Geoffrey, because they both knew well enough that it was Vera's doing, and that Sir Nicholas in his bachelor days would not have dreamed of making such a request. However, they were both hungry by now and only too glad to join the others in the study.

Sir Nicholas waited only long enough to see them both provided with drinks before he asked genially, 'Well, Antony, have you solved your case? Who was the murderer? Not your client, of course.'

'Don't tease the boy, Nicholas,' said Vera gruffly. 'Know he told you he wasn't sure.'

'No, but —' said Antony, and broke off there and sipped his drink in a way that was only too obviously deliberately tantalising.

'You've changed your mind,' said Sir Nicholas, accusing now. 'You'd better tell us what's been said this morning.'

'Have I time?'

'All the time in the world,' said Sir Nicholas. 'Vera's seen to that. And I must admit I'm curious.'

'All right then. Will you oblige, Geoffrey? I've done most of the talking so far.'

'If you like.' He gave a succinct but pretty comprehensive account of the two interviews, but finished rather doubtfully, 'I think that's all.'

'And very clearly expressed indeed,' said Sir Nicholas cordially. 'There's one thing that struck me though, and I'm sure it must have struck you too, Geoffrey. There's some doubt about Antony's intentions —'

'I know what you mean, Sir Nicholas. Whether or not he wants me to call the Dickinsons as witnesses when Jim Arnold is tried?'

'Well, Antony?' his uncle asked.

'Of course I do! But can't you imagine the fuss Dickinson will raise when he knows our intentions. I thought it was simpler to leave the matter open.'

'You mean you thought it was simpler for me to bear the brunt of it when the *subpoenas* are issued,' said Geoffrey. He didn't sound particularly worried.

'In any case,' Maitland pointed out, 'Doctor Dickinson offered —'

'She offered to appear at Prior's trial. That isn't the same thing. And even if *she's* willing, her husband still won't like it. What did you make of his attitude towards her, Antony?'

'I kept changing my mind. First I thought he was loving and over-protective, then he started treating everything she said to a dose of sarcasm. But finally —'

'Well?' said Vera and Jenny together, when he paused.

'I went back to my first impression. I think he gets hurt and annoyed when she won't accept a protective attitude — she's a fairly violent feminist, you know — and that's his way of-hitting back. I don't think he'd be so bitter if he weren't . . . well, almost obsessed by her.'

'Well, be that as it may,' said Geoffrey, 'I don't quite see where it gets us.'

'With the exception of Prior it gets all the men together who might have murdered his wife. If Stan was telling us the truth, and I rather think he was, *he* can't make an identification, and you tell me Alf's refused to say a word so far. But don't you think it might make a difference to him if he comes face to face with his principal and hears him denying all knowledge of the operation, leaving Alf and Stan to face the music alone?'

'Since you ask me,' said Sir Nicholas, 'I don't think it will make any difference at all. If I were running a nefarious enterprise I should arrange beforehand that my subordinates knew they would be looked after in the future so long as they didn't give me away if they were caught.'

'What I think too,' said Vera.

'But it could happen,' said Jenny. 'Perhaps Alf might be a bit awed by being in court. Or perhaps one of these three men might break under cross-examination.'

'Two of them will be your husband's own witnesses, my dear,' Sir Nicholas pointed out. 'However, I admit I should be glad to hear exactly what theory you're working on, Antony. You believe you can get the court to accept that the murder and the extortion are connected?'

141

'I think it's obvious, and I don't think the prosecution will make any real objection. They are two separate cases, and the D.P.P. knows about both of them, but the prosecution at Prior's trial will be relying heavily on evidence about the protection racket.'

'And yet you persist in thinking that Prior was not his wife's accomplice?'

'There was also the other man with whom Joyce Prior was involved.'

'About whom we have heard only from your client himself, and at second-hand from this Charles Shelley you spoke with this morning,' Sir Nicholas pointed out. 'He may or may not exist.'

'I say he does. I think, if you want to know, that the affair had been going on for years, and that Joyce was thoroughly tired of having to hide her feelings. That's why she admitted everything to her husband the moment he accused her, and that's why the other man – whoever he is – felt threatened. And I must admit, Uncle Nick, that I haven't a shred of proof of any of this.'

'You're not proposing, then, to confront one of these men in court with an accusation of guilt?'

'Nothing of the kind,' said Antony hastily. 'Have I ever done that when I wasn't sure?'

'Since I've never known you to become completely confident about anything –'

'You know what I mean, Uncle Nick. I just think there's a chance that in the course of Jim Arnold's trial something may emerge.' He paused and grinned. 'Something really newsworthy,' he said, 'that will have the whole country screaming for justice for Jim Arnold.'

'Not justice, mercy,' Sir Nicholas retorted. 'If you don't know the difference by now it's time you did,' he added.

PART THREE

REGINA *versus* ARNOLD, 1973

THE CASE FOR THE PROSECUTION
WEDNESDAY, The First Day of the Trial

I

As Geoffrey had foretold, the trial came on the following Wednesday, not long before the luncheon recess. Jim Arnold was looking his small, insignificant self, very much as if butter wouldn't melt in his mouth, and Geoffrey, slipping into his seat behind Maitland in the body of the court, said on a note of relief, 'At least we'll have no trouble with him.'

'No,' Antony agreed, 'he knows his way around.' Whether in the long run they would be glad or sorry for that fact was another matter, he had at the moment a more urgent cause for worry. The prosecution were contenting themselves with the bare facts of the case, which left the onus on the defence to call the man who had prepared the report for Cobbolds for instance, and the detective-inspector who had carried matters on from there when it had been delivered to him. Maitland still felt it unlikely that any real objections would be raised to this course of action, but in what should have been a very simple matter the court might be inclined to be unsympathetic towards any complications which lengthened the proceedings unduly. However, that was all for the future, at the moment there was the indictment to be read, after which, not unexpectedly, the judge called the recess.

Mr Justice Conroy was a man of long experience, both on the bench, and before that at the criminal bar. It wasn't the first time Maitland had appeared before him, but without condoning counsel's unorthodox ways (of which he had had first-hand experience, besides being quite familiar with all the legal gossip on the subject) he felt quite capable of controlling matters in his own court. He was, quite unconsciously, an arrogant man, not at all lacking in self-confidence.

When the court reconvened, Counsel for the Prosecution – a

145

man called Hawthorne, of whom Sir Nicholas had the highest opinion, both as an advocate and as a human being – made the briefest of speeches outlining his case. And indeed there wasn't much to be said, though his last words were of more than a little interest to the defence. 'My lord, members of the jury, you will see that the facts in this matter are very clear indeed, subject you will think to only one interpretation. I am given to understand, however, that my learned friend, Mr Maitland, who is appearing for the defence, feels that there are circumstances which entitle the prisoner, James Arnold, to some special consideration. I should like to make it clear, my lord, that the prosecution has no objection to any evidence that may be called to substantiate this point of view.'

Maitland and his junior, Derek Stringer, exchanged a glance, and from Geoffrey Horton came an audible sigh of relief. That meant less argument, perhaps no argument at all, when the defence witnesses were called.

The first prosecution witness, the policeman first on the scene, was already taking the oath. His evidence was a very simple account of the message received to proceed to Kenyon Court, where he found the accused, his pockets stuffed with coins which the owner of the flat claimed as his own; of the subsequent arrival of a police car to ferry the party to the police station, where charges were laid, and Jim Arnold was arrested. He was followed by the divisional detective inspector, who had nothing to add of moment, and Maitland had one question only for each of them in turn.

'Did my client attempt to resist arrest in any way?'

The replies were worded differently, of course, but they amounted to the same thing: Jim Arnold had taken his detention quite quietly, in fact he had seemed almost resigned. 'But he knew the ropes,' the D.D.I. added before anyone could stop him. 'He didn't deny what he'd done, but he didn't have anything to say either, except that he wanted to phone his solicitor.'

Maitland smiled at him. 'As his counsel I was interested in his attitude,' he said. 'That is all, Inspector, unless my learned friend for the prosecution has any further questions.'

Hawthorne hadn't. His next move was to put the coin collection into evidence, to call a fingerprint expert who confirmed that James Arnold had handled them freely, and after him an acknow-ledged expert in such matters to speak to their very considerable value. This man was also able to say that he had known of the collection for many years, and before Henry Franklin retired had tried several times to buy it. Franklin, although keeping the coins at that time in his safe at the shop, consistently refused, saying he regarded them as his own property, not as stock-in-trade, and that they were the one thing he was going to keep when he finally sold the shop. Again the defence had only one question to ask, though this time it was put by Derek Stringer.

'Would you say that the existence of the collection, and Mr Franklin's possession of it, were well known?'

'In the trade perhaps, but only among people who are interested in such things. Coins are my speciality, but if I were interested in jade, for instance, and had heard anyone mention the collection I doubt if it would have stuck in my mind.' As this was precisely the answer Stringer wanted he thanked the witness and seated him-self, only to see Hawthorne on his feet again.

'There is no saying, of course,' he remarked, hardly even pretending that it was a question being put to the witness, 'how many people Mr Franklin may have confided in about this very valuable collection.'

And that, of course, was the sting in the tail of all the evidence about the coins. Antony heaved a sigh of relief when Mr Justice Conroy decided that he had had enough of Jim Arnold's affairs for one day, and adjourned the court until the following morning.

II

When he got back to Kempenfeldt Square the study door was standing open invitingly, and upon investigation he found that Jenny was there with Sir Nicholas and Vera. 'I'll get you a drink,' said Sir Nicholas hospitably as soon as he went in. 'Jenny tells me that nothing very dreadful will happen to your dinner if you stay here for an hour or so, so I thought it would be interesting to hear how your day went.'

'All right, Uncle Nick, but there's nothing really to tell you that you don't know,' said Antony, exchanging a grin with Vera and then sinking down on to the sofa beside his wife.

'Looking tired,' said Vera, in an abrupt way that sounded almost like an accusation.

That was a matter that neither Jenny nor Sir Nicholas would ever have commented on; the pain that his injured shoulder caused him, which could be considerable at times, had been more or less a forbidden subject ever since the doctors had pronounced that nothing could be done about it. But it seemed that it wasn't only with the domestic staff that Vera was capable of rushing in where any self-respecting angel would have feared to tread. Antony only smiled at her quite amiably, shook his head, and then said, 'Discouraged, perhaps.'

'Should have thought it was early days for that,' said Vera bluntly.

'It's Jim Arnold, Vera,' said Antony.

'Know that. Still say −' She broke off there, and added less positively, 'Taken the whole thing very much to heart, haven't you?'

'I suppose I have. And it's not only Jim Arnold though that's the biggest part of it. There's that poor devil Don Tudor, and all the other people Stan and Alf were terrorising.'

'At least,' said Sir Nicholas, 'the − I believe racket is the correct term − the racket has been broken up now. Is there any doubt that these two men who were acting as collectors will go to prison?'

'I shouldn't think so.'

'Well then!'

'What's to stop their principal recruiting some new helpers?'

'He may be imprisoned too,' Sir Nicholas pointed out.

'You mean Archie Prior? That isn't a remark actually calculated to cheer me, Uncle Nick. I think he's innocent.'

'That's more than you can say about Jim Arnold.'

'Yes, I know, but . . . we needn't go into all that again, need we?'

'What happened today? You can't have started putting on your case?'

'No, we're nowhere near that point. We didn't have anything more than the indictment before lunch, and though Hawthorne

148

spoke very briefly we hadn't time for anything but the police evidence and some chat about the coins before Conroy adjourned. Hawthorne won't make any objection to our calling evidence in extenuation, by the way.'

'Then I don't see what you're so depressed about,' said Sir Nicholas frankly.

Antony had his glass by now, and he drank a little sherry before replying. 'He was wonderfully co-operative,' he agreed, 'but he also managed to bring out the one point that cast doubt on Jim's story.'

'I suppose you mean that he may have chosen to rob Franklin because he had heard about the coins and their value,' said Sir Nicholas. 'You can't prove a negative, Antony, and it's no use trying, so you may as well make the best of what you've got.'

'I know that, but —'

'You also know you haven't the faintest chance of proving who Joyce Prior's accomplice was,' Sir Nicholas pointed out. 'That being so —'

'No, Uncle Nick. The most we can hope for is to get Jim off with a lighter sentence than he'd otherwise have got.'

'Which is exactly what I pointed out to you several weeks ago,' said his uncle. 'I suppose you realise, Antony, that if you're right about Archibald Prior being innocent, Henry Franklin is by far the most likely substitute.'

'Oh yes, I realise that all right. Apart from the fact that he handed over the key to the cupboard to Joyce Prior without question, he knew her better than anyone else. What's to say they hadn't had a close relationship all the years she worked for him? But it's no use, you know, I can't prove it and —'

'And you're not at all sure that it's true,' his uncle finished for him.

'No, I'm not.' He picked up his glass again. 'Let's forget the whole beastly business for this evening at least,' he added, but contradicted himself a moment later by saying gloomily, 'And when this is all over there's still Prior's trial to come.'

The next morning brought Henry Franklin to the witness stand, which was of course the first sight Maitland had had of him. He wasn't a tall man, perhaps three or four inches shorter than his wife, and Antony's first thought was that the description he had heard applied to the other man, "a little bit of an old maid", had a good deal of validity. There was a sort of primness about him. All the same, though he might be – like the Shelleys – as grey as a badger, there was no doubt about his good looks; but there was just a little hesitation in his manner that made Maitland wonder what Rita Franklin had seen in him, and seemed still to see in him for that matter.

From Hawthorne's point of view, of course, it was a straight enough story. The value of the coin collection, proof of ownership; a simple enough matter as it had been bought as a whole from another collector, not put together painstakingly through the years. And then the events of the night when Jim Arnold had been caught red-handed making off with his treasure.

'I understand it was only by chance that you were actually at home,' said Hawthorne.

'That's right, we were going to visit my daughter at Barrow-in-Furness. But then I caught a cold and Rita thought –'

'In any case you didn't go, Mr Franklin.'

'No, we didn't. And I'm thankful now. It isn't so much their value, I could have sold them fifty times over before I retired, and even since then there have been some inquiries. But they're so beautiful, I couldn't have borne to think of them in other hands.'

'I gather from what you say, Mr Franklin, that your possession of them was fairly general knowledge.'

'Yes, I think I may say that.'

After that it was mostly repetition, rubbing it well in, thought Antony, but he couldn't blame his learned friend for that. Afterwards Hawthorne sat down with a satisfied air, and Maitland was on his feet.

'I shan't detain you very long, Mr Franklin,' he said, 'but there's one point in your evidence that I should like to have clarified at once. My friend, Mr Hawthorne, asked you whether your posses- sion of the collection of coins which have been produced in evidence was well known. When you replied in the affirmative what exactly did you have in mind?'

'Why, among people interested in such things mainly, I suppose.'

'Other dealers, for instance?'

'Yes certainly. But mainly if their interests ran parallel with mine.'

'I see. That puts rather a different complexion on things, doesn't it?'

'My lord,' said Hawthorne.

'Yes, Mr Maitland, what you're asking the witness is hardly a matter upon which he is competent to judge,' said Mr Justice Conroy gently.

'Certainly not, my lord,' said Maitland in a shocked tone, as though getting an impression over to the jury had been the furthest thing from his mind. 'But among your personal friends, for instance —?'

'I suppose I'm a bit of a bore on the subject but I don't insist on anyone looking at them unless they show an active interest,' said Henry Franklin, less hesitantly than usual.

'I'm sure you're being a little hard on yourself there, Mr Franklin,' Maitland told him. 'Perhaps in the circumstances' – he turned towards the judge – 'your lordship will allow me two questions which call for the opinion of the witness.'

'If you can convince me that it would be proper for me to do so, Mr Maitland.'

'It concerns my client's evidence, my lord, which you will be hearing in due course. If it can be suggested that he broke into Mr Franklin's flat because he already knew of the value of the collec- tion of coins, that would to some extent invalidate his story. As I can hardly call every one of Mr Franklin's friends and business associates to deny having spoke of the matter to Mr Arnold —'

'Heaven forbid,' said the judge piously. 'Ask your questions, Mr Maitland.'

Antony allowed himself one swift glance in Hawthorne's direction, and received a grin in return. 'The question is this, Mr Franklin,' he said turning back to the witness. 'From what you have learned from my client, Mr James Arnold,' (every eye in the court turned towards the prisoner) 'would you think it likely that any of the people with whom you have discussed your collection would have communicated the matter to him?'

'Emphatically, no!' said Henry Franklin, for once quite sure of himself.

'Then let us turn to the next matter. When you – when you apprehended my client did he offer any violence in return?'

'No, nothing of the kind. He did seem a little put out,' said the witness, obviously unconscious of any humour in what he was saying, 'but that I think was natural in the circumstances.'

'Quite natural,' agreed Maitland gravely. 'Did he say anything at all?'

'He offered to turn out his pockets, but I told him not to do that until the police arrived. I think he thought I might agree not to prosecute if he returned what he had taken. He also seemed a little aggrieved to find we were at home, but I explained that just now.'

'But not that my client knew of it. Would you say that meant he had been making some enquiries in the neighbourhood?'

'I thought that was the normal procedure when – er – casing a joint,' said Henry Franklin, obviously proud of this unlikely phrase. For some reason Antony, intent on getting what confirmation he could in advance for Jim Arnold's story, had overlooked this simple point, and seeing his look of consternation his opponent forebore to object.

'Then we come to the question of the key to the cupboard in the downstairs hall at Kenyon Court,' said Maitland, recovering himself. 'Again I must ask your indulgence, my lord. I shall be introducing evidence to show the importance of this cupboard in my client's defence, and my learned friend for the prosecution has already been kind enough to say he'll make no objection.'

'The witness may answer, Mr Maitland.'

'I'm obliged to your lordship. Will you tell us, Mr Franklin, to whom you gave or rented the key to that cupboard?'

'It's under the stairs, quite commodious really. You know when I bought Kenyon Court when I retired, the Dickinsons and the Shelleys were already in occupation, but there was one flat free and Joyce thought it would be very convenient for her and Archie. She said she was nervous in a house when he was away so much.'

'So they took the empty flat?'

'Yes, they did.'

'When exactly was this, Mr Franklin?'

'Three years ago, nearly four.'

'And when was the request made for the use of the cupboard?'

'Oh, Joyce asked me that immediately. Before they definitely said they'd take the flat in fact. You know that was at the time I retired, or rather a few months later, and Joyce was already managing the shop where she had previously been my assistant. She said she sometimes bought pieces on her own account, to hold on to them and sell when the price was right, and there wasn't really room for them in the flat.'

'Weren't you a little surprised she'd want to keep valuables in a place like that?'

'I was, of course. I mentioned the matter to her, but she said, "Who'd think of looking there for anything of value?" And we had a good lock put on, at her expense. There hadn't been one before, I think it had just been used for cleaning materials.'

'Wasn't it rather inconvenient for you to have nowhere to keep them now?'

'No, because Rita thought it was best to employ a firm who'd bring their own materials rather than a charwoman who might be ill from time to time. Anyway that's how Joyce came to have the use of the cupboard, I was very surprised when the police showed it to me after her death and there was nothing in it but a briefcase.'

'That brings us to our final point, Mr Franklin. Did you ever see anybody apart from Mrs Prior going to the cupboard?'

'There may have been a second key, I don't know because as I said she arranged for the lock to be put on. But certainly I never saw anybody else open it.'

'And Mrs Prior?'

'Now that you mention it, it's rather odd I never did see her use it.'

'You know all your tenants, of course. Did you ever see any strangers about?'

'We all have visitors from time to time.'

'Yes, but I'm not thinking of the kind of person who would have been likely to visit you or your tenants.'

'Then let me see. Archie and Joyce were out all day, and so were the Dickinsons. But either the Shelleys or ourselves might have had deliveries made.'

'Let us postulate a time somewhere between seven and eight in the evening.'

'I never saw anybody then, but I wouldn't be likely to. Most evenings I expect Rita and I would be enjoying a drink before dinner at that time.'

'I see. I think that's all, Mr Franklin, I only hope I haven't tried your or the court's patience too much.'

Mr Hawthorne did not wish to re-examine, and that concluded the case for the prosecution.

THE CASE FOR THE DEFENCE
THURSDAY, The Second Day of the Trial

I

'And very nice too,' said Stringer to Maitland, *sotto voce*. 'You're going to have your work cut out to convince them that Jim Arnold had some excuse for what he did.'

'The press are here in force,' said Antony non-committally. Harry Carlton must have spread the word around. He had no idea at all how big a drawing card his own name was.

Derek gave him a rather odd look. 'You're a queer chap,' he said. 'In the normal way that would drive you nearly mad.'

'I explained to you –'

'Yes, I know you did. But to my mind, Antony, it just means that if we make fools of ourselves' (he really meant If you make a fool of yourself, but was generous enough not to say so) 'it will just mean that it will be all the more widely reported.'

'Perhaps I shouldn't have asked you – ' Antony began, and was told roundly not to be a fool. By that time the judge was looking their way and Maitland rose rather hastily to begin his opening address for the defence.

This he had prepared more carefully than usual. It consisted in the main of Jim Arnold's story, but outlined as well the report prepared by the detective from Cobbolds Agency ('naturally, my lord, a good many of their men were concerned in the investigation, and if you wish I'll ask for a recess so that they may all be called.' Mr Justice Conroy's answer to this was eloquent enough, merely a shudder.) Maitland made the same offer of calling additional testimony when the police content of his case was reached. The report had gone to Fulham first, but on realising the ramifications of the matter had been passed to Scotland Yard, and it was one of their men who was waiting to appear. Antony also referred briefly to Stan and Alf, briefly, and cautiously, because he

155

wasn't at all sure what kind of a morass questioning them would lead him into.

'I think all this will lead you, members of the jury,' he concluded, 'to believe that my client was indeed victimised as he will tell you. Now I am not suggesting for a moment that he was right in the assumption he finally reached, after diligent detective work, that Mr Henry Franklin, the witness we have just heard, was the most likely person to be the principal to whom Alfred Gray and Stanley Bond took their day's returns, merely because he was the owner of Kenyon Court. But you must remember that he knew nothing of the cupboard to which Mrs Prior alone had access, he thought the most likely choice was between the two men living on the ground floor, and the fact that Mr Prior was so often away was an additional reason for his deciding on Mr Franklin. The attempted robbery therefore was in the nature of getting his own back, not in the sense in which that phrase is generally used but quite literally.

'I must thank my learned friend, and of course I am extremely obliged to his lordship, for allowing me to present this evidence which might perhaps be considered not strictly relevant to the matter in hand. If justice is to be done, however, I am sure that they and you will realise its importance, and will make every effort to deal charitably with my client's fall from grace. We are attempting to hide nothing from you, in the past James Arnold has seen the inside of prison many times.' (There had been an argument with Geoffrey over admitting that until the time came for sentencing, and now, as he spoke, Antony was assailed with doubt as to whether his decision that the information could be turned to good account was the right one.) 'But in the last seven years, at the earnest urging of his wife, since deceased, he has been working hard and honestly to provide for his family. I am not asking you to condone what he did, but merely to understand how he was driven to it. For the rest, members of the jury, I shall let him speak for himself.'

In the normal way Maitland made his opening address as short as he decently could, and he was rather surprised at this point, and glanced in a startled way at his watch, when the judge called the luncheon recess. He had no idea he'd been speaking for so long.

'I didn't know you had it in you,' said Derek frankly, as they made their way out of the court. 'But you should have saved it for your closing, you know.'

'Perhaps I should. What do you think, Geoffrey? But you see I wanted to catch the attention of the reporters and keep them there,' Antony explained.

'That's all very well if it comes off.'

'Do you think it won't?' He still was anxious but he needn't have worried. When the court reconvened the press was still there in force.

II

But perhaps after all he had spoken at such length that Jim Arnold's evidence came as an anticlimax. Prompted at intervals by his counsel he told his story well, and his rather ineffectual appearance was definitely an asset. Maitland made him stress the fact that he had been afraid for his family's safety, had paid up without argument until after his wife's death, and until he had succeeded in packing his children off out of the country. 'I thought I'd find out who's behind the whole thing if I could, and if I had done I'd have gone to the police,' he asserted. 'But there was just this Stan and Alf I knew about for sure, and if I turned them in and had to give evidence, who's to say I mightn't have been the next victim? But then I was desperate, wanting to join young Jimmy and Doris you know, a chap gets lonely, so I thought it all out and did what seemed best to me. After all, Martha was always the saving kind, I wouldn't have been hard up if it hadn't been for the money I'd had to pay.'

'But you realise now don't you, Mr Arnold,' Antony asked him, 'that your hitting on Mr Henry Franklin as the guilty party was a pure guess and that the circumstances which led you to do so don't in fact exist?'

'If you says so, guv'nor,' said Jim cheerfully. 'I've always found him pretty straight in his dealings with me,' he confided to the court. Mr Hawthorne disappeared behind his handkerchief, but the judge allowed his smile to be seen.

Maitland kept his witness for some time, bringing out again and again the points that he thought might appeal to the sympathy of the jury, but at last it was Hawthorne's turn. 'You spoke of a man who was injured in your neighbourhood, with whom these men who collected money from you said they had dealt because he wouldn't co-operate. What was his name?'

'Mr Maitland said that was something that didn't ought to come out,' said Jim before Antony could speak. 'If this chap, the one that runs the show, isn't caught, he might go after him again.'

'Why should he? The man who was hurt isn't being called to give evidence, is he?'

'My lord,' said Maitland. 'My learned friend's question is entirely reasonable. I can only assure you –'

Again the judge's smile was quite open. 'I think we can take it, Mr Hawthorne,' he said confidentially, 'that Mr Maitland has been on one of the voyages of discovery for which he is notorious. If he has talked to this man, it might indeed be prejudicial –'   .

'Precisely so, my lord.'

'Then we will turn to another matter.'

'You say you made your own investigations, Mr Arnold. They carried you quite a long way. Why didn't you go to the police with the results, and let them find the final solution?'

'A chap like me? I might have got Alf and Stan shopped, but they wouldn't have taken the matter any further. The chap at Kenyon Court would still have been free to ply his wicked trade, and once I'd given evidence, what would have become of me?'

'You have no great opinion of the police, Mr Arnold?'

'Some of them is all right and some of them I wouldn't give the time of day to,' said Jim frankly. 'But just you think about it a minute, guv'nor. I'd have been no better off if I'd gone to them, and I might have been a lot worse.'

'You mean, no better off financially?'

'That's exactly what I do mean.'

'Then let's come to the time when you decided to commit this robbery, Mr Arnold. You say you were prompted by the belief that Mr Franklin was the man who had injured you.'

'I did think so. I see now I was probably wrong.'

'Your grounds for reaching this decision, as outlined first by my friend and then by you, were rather flimsy ones, weren't they?'

'It was the best I could think of.'

'Are you sure, Mr Arnold, that the fact that Henry Franklin was the possessor of a valuable collection of coins had nothing to do with it?'

'I see what you mean, of course, coins are easily portable. But I'd never heard of them and that's the truth.'

'But you knew from your enquiries, did you not, that Mr Franklin had formerly owned an antique shop?'

'Yes, I knew that.'

'Might you not then have supposed that his was the most likely home to be filled with valuable things? He chose that way of making his living, I presume, because he loved and understood old things, would he be likely to live completely bereft of them even after he retired?'

'When you put it like that I have to admit you've got something,' said Jim. 'All the same that wasn't the reason.'

And so it went on. Jim held up his end pretty well, Maitland thought, but his answers were becoming a little ragged as the time wore on. When Hawthorne at last sat down he himself had just one question to repeat, 'You didn't know, did you, Mr Arnold, that there was likely to be anything more valuable in one flat than in another?'

'That's what I've been saying all afternoon, guv'nor,' said Jim, and heaved a sigh of relief when he was able to leave the witness box and go back to the dock.

After that the defence's case proceeded without incident for the rest of the day. Cobbolds' representative, who had prepared their report from information collected by himself and some of his colleagues, had told his story with very little prompting from Derek Stringer and no cross-examination at all, after which the Scotland Yard detective took up the tale, culminating with the arrest of Stan Bond and Alf Gray. At which point the judge himself took a hand in the questioning.

'But surely, Inspector,' he said, putting down his pen and eyeing the witness as closely as though he suspected him of some trickery, 'you didn't leave the matter there. These men have been traced by the agency to which the previous witness belongs as far as Kenyon Court, and your own observations confirmed that. Did you make

159

no enquiries as to their principal?'

'Well, no, my lord. You see the matter was a little ... unusual,' said the witness. 'At that point we were advised that the matter was in the hands of the murder squad, as one of the tenants had been killed and there appeared to be some connection between the two cases.'

Mr Justice Conroy looked all round the court. 'That is the Mrs Joyce Prior of whom we have heard mention,' he said as though to the world at large. And then, turning quickly, 'Is that so, Mr Maitland.'

'That is so, my lord.'

'You may step down,' said the judge to the witness, without consulting counsel on either side. 'Mr Maitland, with Mr Hawthorne's agreement the court has been very patient with you, but I should like to know at this point exactly what you're trying to prove.'

'My lord –'

'Not your client's innocence,' Conroy went on reflectively, ignoring him. 'Neither he nor you have attempted to deny the facts adduced. Not, surely, that he was justified in what he did?'

'Certainly not, my lord. But I felt that if the full facts were known –'

'Ah yes, these extenuating circumstances. I admit the provocation to your client, and that it was perhaps obvious to a man of his background how best he might recoup his finances, but the whole truth? You've shown us part of it, and the afternoon has grown old while we listened. But what of tomorrow? What do you propose?'

'First, my lord, to call these two men, Alfred Gray and Stanley Bond.'

'First?' queried Conroy.

'I have other witnesses to call on, as seems expedient. From Kenyon Court,' he amplified.

'Mr Maitland, this is not an enquiry into the death of Mrs Joyce Prior.'

'I'm aware of the fact, my lord.' Maitland's tone was becoming a little strained. 'I have tried, I think successfully, to establish the proof of the first part of my client's story; if I can also establish the identity of Mrs Prior's accomplice I feel it would go a good way towards establishing the fact that the inference he made, though false, was not altogether unreasonable.'

'Was there an accomplice? And was it necessarily a man?'

'My lord, I have reason to believe that much at least. If you'll permit me –'

'I'll permit you to call one of these two men, Gray or Bond. After that only those people from Kenyon Court who actually saw them there, or who saw Mrs Prior in suspicious circumstances. Is that understood?'

'Your lordship has made the matter perfectly clear,' said Maitland, trying to keep a rebellious note out of his voice. 'May I consult with my instructing solicitor before I reach a decision as to which of the two men I should call?'

'You may have all night to do so,' said the judge cordially. 'Your well-known propensity for – for pulling rabbits out of hats notwith-standing, I think we are all a little weary of the matter.' He got to his feet. 'And for the convenience of those of you who may wish to make other arrangements,' he added, 'I propose to adjourn for the weekend at noon tomorrow. I'm sure,' he added, looking around him, 'that none of you will object to that.'

III

As the court cleared Horton came round to join his two colleagues. Willett was piling papers together, and the solicitor glanced disparagingly at the brief he had so carefully prepared, which now was adorned with a series of scribbles and unlikely looking sketches. One, judging by the wig, might have been his lordship, but if so it was a gross libel.

'I don't know why Hawthorne was so patient with you,' he said abruptly. 'I think Conroy was quite right.'

'A lot of comfort you are,' Antony grumbled. 'All right, Willett, don't wait for me, I'm going straight home. Hawthorne was patient because he's a good fellow and has a sense of justice –'

'And you're known for your propensity to set off fireworks in court,' said Geoffrey, paraphrasing the judge. 'But there won't be any fireworks in this case . . . unless a miracle happens,' he added grudgingly.

161

'Perhaps it will,' said Derek Stringer lightly. For perhaps the thousandth time in their association Antony wondered what his junior was thinking. He could always be sure of Derek's full co-operation in any ploy he himself suggested, but the other man was of a sceptical disposition and it was very likely indeed that most of Maitland's causes left him unmoved.

'If you think that, you're as mad as he is,' said Geoffrey, with a jerk of his head in Antony's direction. 'What are you going to do? I think we should rest our case at this point. You could then make your closing speech in the morning after Hawthorne has had his say, which won't take long. I doubt if the jury will even retire, why should they? We may know the sentence before noon.'

'And what do you think it would be with Conroy in the mood he's in? Heaven knows I didn't mean to get his back up —'

'But you did, and it's no good crying about it now,' said Geoffrey unsympathetically.

'All the same I think we have to go on.'

'And make matters worse . . . witg Conroy I mean?'

'I only know that while there's the faintest chance —' He paused, looking from one to the other of his companions. 'The papers tonight will be running Jim's story, and the fact that it was backed up by both a reputable enquiry agency and the police. There will be omissions of course, because Alf and Stan's trial is coming up. But —'

'You're trading on your reputation,' said Geoffrey unwisely.

'Damn my reputation. Just think, if we could bring it off, if we could expose this man, they'd have half the population weeping into their porridge the next morning over the sad story of Jim Arnold's wrongs.'

'Very well. I don't like it, Antony, and I won't pretend I do, but —'

'I knew I could rely on you.' Antony's mood changed immediately. 'The witnesses we're allowed from Kenyon Court are limited to the two Dickinsons and Charles Shelley. Not that I think Rita Franklin could have helped any further, or Alfreda Shelley for that matter. As for the two collectors, the one I want to call is Alf Gray.'

'But he's the one who won't talk.' Geoffrey's voice went up in protest. 'Surely it would be better —'

162

'All Stan can tell us is what Cobbolds and the police have discovered for themselves. Besides he doesn't know the man who employed them, Alf at least saw him.'

'Have it your own way.' Geoffrey was growing exasperated again.

'Then that's settled.' Derek sounded relieved. 'What you really want, Antony,' he added, trying to introduce a lighter note as he urged them on their way, 'is Joyce Prior's evidence. Why don't you consult this medium friend of yours?'

But Maitland was in no mood to be amused. 'I would if I thought it would do any good,' he snapped and left with the curtest of goodbyes.

IV

He walked home and took his time about it, but his problem seemed no nearer to solution when he arrived. Again, as seemed to be becoming a habit, the study door stood open, but he was about to ignore its invitation when Gibbs came forward to tell him Mrs Maitland was with Sir Nicholas and Lady Harding. At that he changed his direction and went in to join them.

To his surprise, nothing was said immediately, except by way of greeting. That was explained when they were all settled with their drinks. 'Halloran tells me,' said Sir Nicholas, holding up his glass and eyeing the pale straw-coloured sherry with approval, 'that Mr Justice Conroy is not altogether sympathetic with this latest quirk of yours.' Bruce Halloran, Q.C., was an old friend of Sir Nicholas's, a man with an information service second to none in the legal fraternity.

'If you know so much,' said Antony tiredly, 'you won't want any further account from me.'

'No, I think his story today was fairly comprehensive,' said Sir Nicholas thoughtfully. 'And Geoffrey, I imagine, has been urging you to give up at this point.'

'You're quite right, Uncle Nick, he has. I suppose you're going to tell me the same thing.'

163

'Your business,' said Vera gruffly. Jenny who was sitting beside her husband on the sofa reached out a hand to touch his gently.

'I agree with Vera, of course,' said Sir Nicholas, 'but am I to gather that you refused his suggestion?'

'Yes, I did.'

'That can only be because you feel there's still some small chance of being successful.'

'I think "small chance" is an exaggeration, sir.' Antony attempted to smile. 'But I couldn't live with myself if I gave up while there was any chance at all.'

'Then there's just one thing I must point out to you.'

'I think it would make all the difference to Jim's chances if we could expose the – the chief extortionist,' said Antony stubbornly.

'And I'm not arguing with you about that, my dear boy. The newspapers would have what I believe my dear wife would call a field day, and Conroy of all people is not immune to public opinion. But have you considered what the position would be if your prying were to disclose the fact that your other client, Archibald Prior, is guilty both of extortion and murder?'

'I don't think that's true.'

'But if it is?' Sir Nicholas insisted.

'I should have made an unforgivable mistake in accepting Prior as a client.'

'If you mean a mistake that your legal brethren couldn't forgive, I think you're wrong about that. Your reputation would stand you in good stead.'

'Geoffrey was talking about my reputation, but he didn't mean exactly that.'

'No, I can imagine. And you were telling me that you wouldn't forgive yourself, but that too is beside the point. What I want you to consider is the capital Chief Superintendent Briggs could make of it.'

'He couldn't turn an error of judgment into a crime.'

'I'm not so sure. If he could persuade the D.P.P. that you would deliberately sacrifice one client for another –'

'But why should I do that?'

'I know there's no reason, my dear boy, you don't have to argue the matter with me. But there's our previous association with Jim

164

Arnold to consider, and the fact that the purchase of Mrs Arnold's shop can be traced to me.'

Antony was sitting bolt upright now and looking appalled. 'Uncle Nick, you're not trying to say there could be a scandal that would involve you as well as me?'

'No, I don't think so. Don't worry your head about that, Antony. It will be assumed that you persuaded me into the purchase by telling me some concocted story.'

'But it's so simple, we had reason to be grateful to Mrs Arnold and there was the fact too that we'd deprived Jim of his pension fund, even if it was an illegal one.'

'Is anyone going to believe that? I may be supposed to have done so, but I think the more likely interpretation put on your actions would be that Jim Arnold – whom you've known for a very long time, may I remind you? – has some hold over you, and that is why you are trying desperately now to do your best for him.'

'They couldn't prove that,' said Antony flatly.

'No, but the mere fact that the charge was made . . . I wouldn't entertain this idea for a moment, Antony, if it weren't for Briggs's animosity. As it is I have to admit I'm very worried indeed.'

Antony took his time to look at each of his companions in turn. 'Vera's worried, Jenny's worried, and I'm worried. All the same, I don't think I can turn back now.'

'That means you've got some idea in your head –'

'Of course he has, Uncle Nick,' said Jenny, suddenly joining in the conversation. 'You know Antony always has ideas, and nearly always they're right.'

'Operative word is nearly,' said Vera.

'Precisely, my dear.' Sir Nicholas sounded triumphant, but he was solemn enough when he turned back to his nephew again. 'And what is this idea of yours, Antony?' he asked.

'That I know the name of the man who employed Alf and Stan, the man who was Joyce Prior's lover and accomplice, and who murdered her at last.'

'The same man?'

'Yes, I think that goes without saying.' He got to his feet and held out his left hand to pull Jenny to hers. 'We have to go now Vera,' he added with the slight touch of formality he still used sometimes towards her. 'Meg had to be early at the theatre for some meeting or other, so Roger's coming to dinner. We ought to be there to greet him.'

'Got an idea I know what Meg's meeting is about,' said Vera, when Antony and Jenny had departed.

'Do you, Vera? I had supposed some sort of an extra rehearsal.'

'No, there's talk of their taking the play to America.'

'I thought it was all set for a long run here.'

'Yes, the whole cast wouldn't go. Meg's understudy would take over for six weeks and she'd start the play off in New York. That's about as long a permit as she could get, I understand, a couple of weeks for rehearsals and a month in the theatre. Roger says he's going with her.'

'That will be nice for them both. My dear you're being unusually loquacious about this.'

'Have an idea,' said Vera. 'Might do Jenny and Antony good to have a holiday.'

'It might indeed, but what are you proposing should happen to the cases Antony has on hand?'

'Christmas vacation,' said Vera laconically. 'Know it's a long way off yet, but can't see it would do anything but good —'

'To get him out of Briggs's way for a while,' Sir Nicholas completed the sentence for her. 'Does that coincide with the time Meg and Roger will be away?'

'They'll be there rehearsing for a fortnight — at least Meg will — before *Done in by Daggers* opens on New Year's Day. Antony and Jenny could have nearly three weeks away and be back in time for the Hilary Term.'

'You're working on the principle, out of sight, out of mind, aren't you, my dear? Well, if nothing disastrous happens during Jim Arnold's trial —'

'Don't think it will.'

'Why not, Vera?'

'Can't make bricks without straw. Antony's got his own ideas and he may well be right, but Conroy has tied his hands effectively.'

'Let's hope you're right, my dear.'

'Any case, think the change will do them good,' Vera insisted.

'Can you persuade Jenny –?'

'In this case I think Meg might be the better ally,' said Sir Nicholas and smiled as he spoke. 'I can quite see her telling them perfectly convincingly that she couldn't possibly think of opening in a foreign country without some friendly faces about her. And making them believe it too,' he added, and for the first time that day there was amusement in his tone.

Geoffrey Horton got to court early the next day, to have a word both with the first witness and with their client before the proceedings started. 'Jim's pretty cheerful,' he reported when he joined his colleagues in court. 'He thinks he'll get a lightish sentence and seems to be resigned as to the consequences.'

'And Alf?'

'Sullen, as you'd expect. I pointed out to him, of course, that helping us wouldn't prejudice his position, but might even help it, but I think my words fell on deaf ears. You're going to have to be damn careful about this, Antony.'

'I'll be careful,' Antony promised. He had spent a bad night and looked it, and was afraid that Jenny had too, but he was glad to see that, as he had expected, Geoffrey was again his usual helpful self. The judge entered at that moment and there was no chance for further conversation. A few moments later Maitland got to his feet again to address Alf Gray, who had arrived under guard and was now in the witness box.

As Geoffrey had said, he had a sulky look, but he managed somehow to maintain the neatness that Jim Arnold had described so graphically. After the preliminaries were over – he gave his occupation as businessman – he looked straight at Maitland and remarked disagreeably, 'It's you, is it? Well I tell you straight I don't know why I'm here. I've got nothing to tell you.'

'Mr Gray,' said Antony cautiously – the witness was tricky, and so was the situation – 'let me first make it very clear to you that we have no desire to embarrass you in any way. Our only interest is in a man who approached you in a public house one evening some five years ago with a – shall we say with a business proposition?'

'Me memory doesn't go back that far.'

'Does it not? Yet this man, I believe, became your employer.'

'If you likes to put it that way.'

'What was his name?'

168

'Never knew it.'

'His appearance then.'

'Don't remember.'

'Was that occasion five years ago the only time you saw him?'

'We was in communication when necessary,' said Alf with dignity. 'No need to meet.'

'I'm not going to ask you about your work, Mr Gray. You would be entitled, and quite rightly, to decline to answer. But it would be helpful to know a little about these communications. They contained explicit directions as to the work you were to undertake for your employer, did they not?'

'What if they did?'

'Did they, Mr Gray, or didn't they? My impression is that you and your partner would not have been content with a small cut in the takings of this business enterprise of yours unless these instructions were of some specific benefit to you.' Alf was silent, and Maitland continued persuasively after a moment, 'Come now, Mr Gray, you describe yourself as a businessman. I'm sure you had a very good idea of what your services were worth.'

'Well then, I did. And the chap we're talking about knew how many beans made five, no mistake about that.'

'Mr Maitland?' said the judge.

'I take the witness to mean that his employer was knowledgeable concerning their activities, my lord. Is that right, Mr Gray?'

'Right enough.'

'I see. Thank you, Mr Maitland.' Conroy leaned back again.

'So that brings us back,' said Antony, 'to the question I asked you before. Can you describe this gentleman to us?'

'No.'

'You don't remember anything about his appearance? Whether he was tall, short, fat or thin, for instance?'

'Not a thing.'

And that, although Maitland continued stubbornly until everyone in the court must have been as weary as he was of his questions, was all that the witness could be induced to say. At last counsel gave up. 'That is all I have to ask you for the moment, Mr Gray,' he said. 'Unless my learned friend for the prosecution has some questions for you —'

Before Hawthorne could indicate his intentions the judge pounced. 'All you have to ask "for the moment", Mr Maitland?' he demanded ominously.

'My lord, I was about to make a request. I realise, of course, that in the circumstances it is not altogether convenient for this witness to be kept in court, but I should be very much obliged if this could be done, at least until the jury retire.'

'Are you indicating that you intend to ask him still more questions?' asked Conroy, as one fearing the worst.

'No, my lord. If I ask anything it will be one question only.'

'Can you guarantee that, Mr Maitland?'

'Cross my heart and hope to die,' said counsel, momentarily forgetting himself. Someone had used the phrase to him recently, and his instinct for mimicry, though unconscious, was always strong.

'Very well.' Mr Justice Conroy inclined his head. 'Have you any questions for the witness, Mr Hawthorne?'

'Not one, my lord.'

'I'm afraid Mr Maitland will think me unkind if I say, thank heaven for that,' said the judge. 'I gather, however, from your request,' he added, turning to Antony, 'that you have not yet completed your case.'

'Your lordship agreed –'

'Yes, certainly. How many people fall within the category I mentioned?'

'Three, my lord.'

'Then we shall certainly not finish today.'

'No, my lord, I'm afraid not.'

'Oh well! Into each life some rain must fall,' remarked the judge in a resigned tone. 'Call your next witness, Mr Maitland.'

But Antony, in the brief interval while Alf Gray vacated the witness box and Mamie Dickinson took his place, turned a despairing look on Geoffrey. 'You were right,' he said. 'We ought to have called Stan. I should have known that one was as stubborn as a mule.'

'He might still make an identification. That's what you're hoping for, isn't it?'

'Only if he's convinced that he and Stan have been thrown to the wolves and the other chap's getting off scot free,' said Antony.

170

'And how am I to convey that to him, I ask you, within the limits Conroy has set me? Still,' he added, not quite so despondently, 'there was one small point –'

'Do you want to examine Doctor Dickinson, or shall I?' asked Derek, beside him. 'She's been sworn and I think Conroy is growing impatient.'

'Good lord! Thank you, Derek, but I think I'd better.' He was on his feet as he spoke, eyeing the witness, wondering whether his earlier impression of her had been the right one. 'Tell me, Doctor Dickinson,' he began, when she had answered his preliminary questions, 'whether Mr Henry Franklin ever spoke to you about his collection of coins?' And that was something surely that even Conroy couldn't object to.

'Oh yes, indeed.' Her eyes sought out Henry Franklin, where he sat among the witnesses who had already given their evidence. 'I was interested, you see. I think a lot of people here, and in Europe generally, don't appreciate all the old things as they should.' She paused a moment, but it was obvious that she hadn't quite finished what she had to say, and Maitland made no attempt to interrupt. 'Henry could tell me the history of every one of the coins, and he has a very inventive mind, you know. Sometimes that history suggested a whole fictitious tale to him of who the owners might have been and what their lives were like. I found it fascinating.'

'Yes, I understand,' (Another answer he could have done without.) 'Am I to gather from that that you discussed the matter among your friends, that perhaps the knowledge of the coins might have been obtained from someone to whom you spoke of them?'

'Oh no, I didn't mean that for a moment,' she said hurriedly, and Maitland heaved a sigh of relief. 'Henry didn't even discuss them with Rufus, he isn't interested in things like that. Unless perhaps,' she added, smiling to herself, 'if Henry had sold them he might have been thinking about capital gains tax, something like that.'

'And you didn't mention them to anybody else?'

'No, I think I can be quite sure about that. Nobody at all.'

'Thank you.' (Never push your luck.) 'Now I understand that you and your husband already lived at Kenyon Court before Mr Franklin bought the building?'

171

'Yes, we were there at least three years before. As a matter of fact we were rather concerned about the change of ownership, you never know what sort of a landlord you'll get. I even suggested to my husband that he buy the place himself, but he didn't seem to want to be tied down. And then we've been there all this time.'

'Mr and Mrs Shelley?'

'Oh, they were there even before we were, but I know they never considered buying. Alfreda can't wait until Charles is due for retirement. I don't think he minds much himself either, and they want to go and live in the country.'

'What I was leading up to, Doctor Dickinson,' said Maitland with a rather wary eye on the judge, 'was to ask you if you remembered Mr and Mrs Prior moving in.'

'Oh yes, of course, not long after the Franklins took over. They were friends, you know, and Joyce worked for Henry.'

'Yes. It's about Joyce Prior I want to speak to you. Of course you're familiar with the cupboard under the stairs in the hall at Kenyon Court.'

'I knew there was one there, of course, but I never noticed it particularly.'

'You didn't know, then, that Mrs Prior had a key to that cupboard?'

'Not until after she was killed.'

'Mr Maitland,' said the judge, 'may I remind you –'

'I apologise to your lordship. Doctor Dickinson, we're not now concerned with Mrs Prior's unfortunate decease. But that cupboard and the possession of the key is material to the case that is now being heard. Did you ever see her go to it?'

'No, but I dare say I never should have done if she wanted to keep the matter secret,' said Mamie Dickinson, thinking it out as she spoke. 'If I was coming down the stairs for instance, she could hear me and pretend either to be going back into her own flat or out of the front door.'

'Yes, that's true. There's just one more thing I have to ask you, then. Did you see anyone come into the building at Kenyon Court at any time who seemed, let us say, a little out of place there? Not likely to be on visiting terms with any of your fellow tenants?'

'Yes, I did.'

'On many occasions?'

'Yes, quite a number of times, but always the same two men.'

'Do you see either of them here in court?'

She took her time to look around her. 'Yes, the big man sitting over there,' she said, pointing to Alf Gray.

'Did you ever see them before the Priors and the Franklins moved in?'

'Not so far as I recall.'

'But since then —?'

'I suppose five or six times. Always when I came home late, as I sometimes do, between seven-thirty and eight I'd say.'

'Can you describe these occasions?'

She frowned over that. 'There's nothing much to describe about them,' she said at last. 'I might be on the stairs going up to our flat when they came in, or I might follow on their heels. In either instance they behaved in exactly the same way, going from one door to the other on the ground floor and peering at the name-plates beside the door as though they were looking for someone. I just presumed they were delivering something and never gave it another thought.'

'You never saw them go near the cupboard?'

'No.'

'Was either of them carrying anything?'

'The big man carried a small black attaché case, but they might have had a truck outside, of course, that was what I thought. And then I wondered if perhaps they were door-to-door salesmen, but they never came upstairs.'

'Then all I can do is thank you for your help, Doctor Dickinson, and —'

'Mr Maitland!' She interrupted him urgently. 'There's something that's been worrying me ever since you talked to me before, something I ought to have told you.'

Antony didn't much believe in intuition, but at that moment he was gripped by a premonition of disaster. 'I think perhaps we should go into that at another time and place, madam,' he said, but it was too late for that. Mr Justice Conroy was leaning forward.

'I have indulged your whims to quite a considerable extent, Mr Maitland. Now I think you must allow us to hear what this lady has

173

to say.'

'My lord, our interview concerned quite a different matter.'

'Nevertheless –' said Conroy inexorably.

Maitland turned back to the witness and tried to smile at her. Somehow in spite of his own panic he had a feeling that she too was in need of reassurance. 'Very well, Doctor Dickinson, what did you wish to tell me?' he asked.

'It was about the telephone call to Archie Prior telling him Joyce was playing around,' said Mamie miserably. '*I* made it, or rather I got my receptionist to make it for me. I made her believe it was some kind of joke. And I've been ashamed about it ever since.'

Mr Justice Conroy was looking like a thundercloud. 'You were quite right, Mr Maitland, it is none of our concern, and I can only apologise to you, madam, for putting you through this ordeal. And now, Mr Hawthorne, if you have any questions for this lady I must ask you to defer them. The court is hereby adjourned until Monday morning.'

II

'So you see, Uncle Nick,' said Antony, having been fortunate enough to find Sir Nicholas alone at their favourite table at Astroff's at lunch-time, 'you're quite entitled to say I told you so. Things are just about as bad as they could be. And what she said won't go into the record, of course, but everyone knows now that Archie Prior had every reason to be angry with his wife and to mistrust her too.'

'But you're still convinced of his innocence,' said Sir Nicholas, signalling a waiter and ordering a double whisky without consulting his nephew's wishes.

'More than ever.'

'Even coming from you that must mean something,' said his uncle.

'Only that this idea I had ... one or two things seem to confirm it.'

'Do you want to tell me about it?'

'Uncle Nick, you're scaring me stiff.' He would have stopped

174

there, but his uncle's bewildered stare obviously required some explanation of him. 'All this gentle forbearance,' he said.

Sir Nicholas smiled in a grim way rather reminiscent of his wife. 'Vera and I have tried to impress upon you a number of times, without success, the seriousness of this obsession of Briggs's,' he observed.

'Yes, I know that, Uncle Nick, and I know that the situation you warned me about last night has come to pass. In trying to help Jim Arnold I seem to have scuttled another client, who is being held on a far more serious charge. But I still think, given the circumstances, I did the only possible thing.'

'Do you want to tell me about it?' asked Sir Nicholas again.

'Guesswork, Uncle Nick,' Antony reminded him.

'I am, however, willing to listen.' And when Maitland still hesitated his uncle went on, 'May I remind you that your aunt and I, not to mention Jenny, may be said to have a personal stake in your well-being.'

'It's only . . . Uncle Nick, if you tell me my ideas are all nonsense I've nothing left to hold on to.'

'*He either fears his fate too much*,' said Sir Nicholas. 'I hope I needn't complete the quotation for you, Antony.'

'No, you needn't.' He smiled suddenly. 'I believe those lines were written as a love poem,' he said.

'Never mind that. You've had some idea in your mind from the very beginning or you'd never have embarked on this crazy crusade. Now you tell me one or two things tend to confirm it. Well?'

'It was natural that I had my doubts about Jim Arnold's story from the beginning,' said Antony. 'But first the fact that the protection racket existed was confirmed, and then the further details he gave about the connection with Kenyon Court. Jim knew nothing of the cupboard, but Cobbolds' report told me about that, though it wasn't until after Joyce Prior was killed that I knew that she was the only person known to have access to it. But there was Stan's story, that his friend Alf had been approached by a man. It seemed likely that her accomplice, if she had one, was therefore a member of the opposite sex. I began to think very hard about all the four men who lived in the building. Prior was the obvious choice, because, besides having a motive rather stronger than the others because there was no doubt a divorce was under way, he had a better opportunity than most. But I couldn't accept it as impossible that one of the other tenants had seen the tablets in his bathroom cupboard and either known or made it their business to find out what they were. So that threw the field wide open.'

'As far as you were concerned,' Sir Nicholas murmured.

'Yes, I like Prior and I wanted to believe his story. When he comes to trial I shall . . . I should have . . . shall I be defending him, Uncle Nick?'

'Leave that for the moment. Tell me what you intended to do.'

'I should have tried to stop him from blurting out that he was the injured party in the divorce. If he'd been the one that wanted to be free, that would have reduced his motive by at least a little. But now, of course, what Mamie Dickinson said in court puts that right out of the question. *He* was the one with a cause for grievance.'

'Yes, I had realised that,' said Sir Nicholas, rather dryly.

'I'm sorry, sir, I meant to be chronological but I seem to have got side-tracked. Then, as Jim had done, I considered Henry Franklin. He knew Joyce better than anyone else there, and could well have been her accomplice, and perhaps her lover if Prior were telling the truth. He, if anyone, was in a position to know the cupboard's possibilities, and to dispose of the key where he chose. On the other hand, I had the impression that he and his wife were genuinely fond of one another, but that's a thing it's difficult to be sure about.'

'It is, indeed. So we come to the other two men. And there's a difficulty here, Antony, as I see it. According to everything we've heard the extortion was going on before Kenyon Court changed hands and became Henry Franklin's property. If one of those two – what are their names? Dickinson and Shelley? – was the man behind it all, what did he do before Joyce Prior came on the scene and made the cupboard available to him?'

'There's nothing to say that one of them didn't know her before she and her husband moved to Kenyon Court. It would be an additional reason for her pressing for the move. Jim Arnold's investigations, let me remind you, only started after his two children went to Canada, between two and two-and-a-half years ago. We don't know where Alf and Stan may have been depositing the money before that, and I didn't have the sense to ask Stan that question when I had the chance.'

'You can't think of everything,' said his uncle unexpectedly. 'However, in the case of one of these two men, what do you think happened before the Priors moved to Kenyon Court?'

'Archie Prior is away, quite often out of the country, for long stretches at a time. Joyce Prior might quite well have been the receiver right from the beginning . . . don't you think?'

'I suppose it's possible. Some different arrangement might have been made while Prior was at home.'

'Of course it might. They might have used a locker at one of the stations, for instance; we're looking back to a time before all the bomb scares. But however it was I think you'll agree, Uncle Nick, they were possibles and couldn't be overlooked.'

'I'll agree to anything if it will make you get on with your story,' said Sir Nicholas a little testily.

The whisky had arrived some time since and had remained untouched at his elbow. Now Antony picked it up and drank rather as if he were thirsty, apologising when he saw Sir Nicholas eyeing him with a little alarm. 'All right, Uncle Nick. I needed that but I'm not taking to drink. And I'm sorry to be so slow about it, but my ideas unfolded slowly, if I may put it that way.'

'Go on,' said his uncle, resigned.

'I may as well tell you that I'm ruling Charles Shelley out of it right away. He isn't the type, he and his wife are a devoted couple looking forward to their retirement, and I think their needs are simple.'

'That might be an elaborate deception,' said Sir Nicholas seriously.

'You're pulling my leg, Uncle Nick. I'll admit to you now that Archie Prior and Henry Franklin remain possibilities, both as extortioner and murderer; I think you'll admit that the two roles go together.'

'I don't like coincidences any better than you do, Antony.'

'No, I thought not. But as to what I *think*.' He stressed the word slightly. 'My first clue came when I was talking to Stan, and he said he and Alf had always received detailed instructions, who to threaten and exactly how much money to demand for their victims' so-called protection. I gathered from Jim Arnold that the demands gauged almost to a penny what he could afford without actually going into debt. Don't you think that argues some special knowledge?'

'I see where your mind is going, of course, and I admit it's ingenious. Rufus Dickinson is a senior civil servant in the Department of Inland Revenue.'

'Exactly. Don't you think he could have known, or made it his business to find out, which of the shops were doing well, which men could afford to pay? Besides there'd be the matter of allowances, he'd know what family they had, what threats could be made against their wives and children most effectively. It all fits in, Uncle Nick. Alf and Stan would never have been content with a comparatively small share of the takings if they hadn't been getting value for money in the information that was handed to them.'

'I like that point,' said Sir Nicholas.

'Well, what Alf said today only went to confirm it. I told you about that. And then there's the drug used. Dickinson's wife is a doctor, and showed quite clearly when I talked to them that she was familiar with its properties. If one or other had seen the bottle by chance they might easily have discussed it. But it was that last disastrous remark of Mamie Dickinson's that really clinched the matter in my mind. Oh God, Uncle Nick, I've been suspecting him for ages, but what happened today was quite unexpected, and I don't know how to deal with it.'

'You say it confirmed your suspicions?'

'You haven't met her, Uncle Nick, I have. She's not very popular with the other people in the apartment because they don't understand her, and I admit she has some ideas that neither you nor I would endorse. But she isn't a mischief maker and she'd never have done a thing like getting her receptionist to call Archie Prior without some very good reason.'

'If you're right about that —'

'I think she found out,' said Antony, ignoring the fact that his uncle was obviously one jump ahead of him at this stage, 'that her husband was playing fast and loose with Joyce Prior, and I think for all she pretends to be so hard-boiled it hurt her as badly as it would hurt any woman. She made that phone call out of injured pride, and I think she's right when she says she's been regretting it ever since. But I don't suppose she has the faintest idea that her husband's connection with Joyce Prior included being her accomplice in the extortion racket.'

'Even so —'

'Don't you see, Uncle Nick, however much playing around Dickinson's done I think he's in love with his wife. Joyce may have been pressing for marriage, he wouldn't like that and may have been just waiting for an opportunity to get rid of her. Trying to implicate Prior would give him a motive for seeing if he had anything that could be stolen and used, and then the calling together of the tenants gave him opportunity, an opportunity, moreover, that wasn't exclusive to him.'

'Did you ask Doctor Dickinson —?'

'And have Conroy jumping all over me again?'

'You haven't been displaying too much concern about that. Consideration for the lady's feelings, however —'

'Have it your own way,' said Antony hastily.

'So what do you propose to do?' asked Sir Nicholas.

Antony smiled rather drearily 'To trade quotation for quotation. Uncle Nick, *I am in blood stepp'd in so far that, should I wade no more, returning were as tedious as go o'er.*'

'Taken in context, that's no more apt than mine was,' Sir Nicholas pointed out. 'But I see your point all the same. The damage is done and you may as well continue as you intended. Will you call Doctor Dickinson back to the stand?'

'You mean to try to make her tell me why she caused the phone-call to be made? I thought of that of course, Uncle Nick, but I couldn't bring myself to do it even if Conroy would stand for it. She's a nice person, and if I'm right she's going to be hurt damnably.'

'If you're right, and if you can prove it,' Sir Nicholas said.

'No, whether I can prove it or not. She isn't a fool and she'll realise sooner or later that the two things are joined together. How do you think she'll feel then?'

'If your sensibilities won't admit you to recall her, what do you mean to do?' asked his uncle, ignoring the question.

'Call Rufus Dickinson. I haven't a hope of tripping him up, because Conroy will jump all over me if I step out of line for a moment.'

'One small doubt remains in my mind. Why did Dickinson admit having seen Joyce Prior carrying an attaché case?'

'Because others might have seen her, and remembered that they often left the building at the same time. He couldn't know it would lead to his being one of the exceptions to Conroy's ban on further witnesses.'

'I understood you also have the option of calling Charles Shelley.'

'Yes, but what's the good? No, Uncle Nick, I'll call Dickinson and then I'll call it a day. As for representing Archie Prior any further, you and Vera can tell me what to do about that. I'm past making up my mind.'

'The trouble with you is,' said Sir Nicholas, suddenly energetic, 'that you've imbibed a large quantity of alcohol on an almost empty stomach.' He turned to signal to the waiter and ordered, again without consulting his nephew, the most substantial thing on the menu which happened to be steak and kidney pie. 'You'll feel better when you've eaten,' he assured Antony kindly. But he added a little later to Vera that he thought all of them were in for a very unpleasant weekend.

MONDAY, *The Fourth Day of the Trial*

Sir Nicholas had been quite right, the weekend was difficult for all of them, enlivened only by Roger and Meg, who came to tea on Sunday as they so often did, and stayed on to dinner. Meg was full of her coming visit to the United States. 'Roger's coming with me for the whole six weeks, darlings,' she said. 'He says any of his clients who want his advice can jolly well telephone.' (Roger was a stockbroker.) 'Well, as a matter of fact he said something worse about them.' She cast down her eyes demurely. 'But I don't like to tell you with Uncle Nick here.'

'Do you know, Meg, I think I might be able to bear it,' said Sir Nicholas, amused.

'Well, it doesn't matter anyway. You see I've been thinking, darlings,' – she was dividing her words between Antony and Jenny now, and no-one could have told from her demeanour that it wasn't a perfectly spontaneous idea – 'why don't you come across for the Christmas vacation? Part of the time I'd be rehearsing and have the evenings free, and then it would be wonderful for Roger to have your company when we open.'

'That's a wonderful idea.' Jenny was immediately enthusiastic. 'Don't you think so, Antony?'

'I do, of course. There's nothing I'd like better. Wait a bit before you start packing though, love, let's see how things go.'

'But you will think about it,' Meg insisted.

'Yes, of course.' He smiled at her warmly. 'It's just that I have things on my mind just now.'

And perhaps, he reflected as he made his way to court on the Monday morning, the worst thing about the weekend had been the failure of Sykes to telephone. There had been occasions in the past when the detective had seen fit to warn him of the possible consequences of his actions; Antony regarded him as a friend, and the only reason for his failure to communicate on this occasion must be that he felt things had already gone too far.

Geoffrey Horton and Derek Stringer both looked subdued. Each of them had suggested a conference during the weekend, but after his talk with Sir Nicholas Antony had told them flatly there was nothing to discuss. They wouldn't be recalling Dr Dickinson. Rufus Dickinson would be their last witness, and then they'd call it a day.

'It isn't like you, Antony,' Geoffrey had said worriedly.

Derek, with his habit of acquiescence to his leader's whims, had said only, 'If that's what you want,' and probably forgotten about the matter altogether, thought Antony with a little bitterness, for the rest of the weekend. Which was unfair to a man who had followed him without question in and out of a good deal of trouble, so he banished the thought from his mind and prepared to face the witness. And to his horror he found that his mind had gone completely blank. He couldn't remember that ever happening before in court. He had a habit of concentrating on the witness he was questioning to the exclusion of anything else, and now that it was absolutely vital . . .

The formula of question and answer which must precede every examination steadied him. And as he might have foreseen from Geoffrey's account of Dickinson's reaction to the *subpoena* the witness was glowering at him with every evidence of hatred. That might perhaps be turned to good account.

'Mr Dickinson –' he started.

'I should like to get it on record,' said Rufus Dickinson, speaking loudly to override counsel's voice, 'that I consider it an iniquitous waste of my time and of the court's time to have called me here at all. I know nothing of the burglary. As for distressing my wife –'

'Mr Maitland,' said Conroy mildly. Dickinson had at least the grace to break off his tirade when the judge spoke. 'You really must keep your witness in better order.'

'If your lordship pleases,' said Maitland meaninglessly. 'Perhaps it will satisfy you, Mr Dickinson, if I assure you that I am quite convinced that you indeed know nothing of the theft of Mr Franklin's coins.'

'Then what the devil do you want of me?'

'Mr Maitland,' sighed the judge.

'Yes, my lord. Would it be premature to ask permission to regard the witness as hostile?'

'He certainly seems to have taken a dislike to you,' said Conroy with a tight little smile. 'However, you'll recall, Mr Maitland, that I gave permission for these further witnesses only on sufferance. As you've seen fit to take advantage of my – I can only say my lenience, I don't think the question of treating one of your own witnesses as hostile can really arise.'

'If your lordship pleases,' said Maitland again. 'I have a very good reason for calling you, Mr Dickinson,' he added, turning back to the witness. 'Of course, you've not been present during the previous part of the hearing –'

'Cooped up in a stuffy room when I could have been better employed elsewhere.'

'Yes, precisely. In the circumstances I must trespass on the patience of the court to tell you very briefly about my client's defence.'

'Shouldn't think he had one,' said Dickinson gruffly.

'That, Mr Dickinson, is a most improper remark,' said Maitland, deliberately provoking. 'If you'll be good enough to listen to me –'

'I suppose I must.'

'I think you must. His lordship will tell you –'

'Very well then.'

'My client has admitted his fault –'

'His crime,' the witness corrected him.

'Very well, his crime. In extenuation he offers the fact that he has for several years been the victim of extortion, that is, he has been offered so-called protection in return for sums of money. As threats were made against his family he did nothing about this until his wife died and he had persuaded his two children to leave the country. Then he traced the two men who called on him regularly to collect the money to Kenyon Court, where you live. Being in desperate need of money and unable to put up his shop for sale for reasons which I imagine are obvious, he decided on the dreadful expedient of robbery to furnish his needs, and – mistakenly, I am sure – decided that perhaps your landlord, Mr Henry Franklin, was the most likely person to be master-minding the operation, and that to steal from him would therefore have a sort of rough justice about it.'

'Henry? That's a laugh. But these chaps will say anything.'

'It has been suggested, however, that his motive in picking on Mr Franklin might have been a more mercenary one, that he knew of the collection of coins and their value.'

'I should think that very likely.'

'I must therefore ask you whether you knew of the collection.'

'Of course I did. It was Henry's favourite subject.'

'Did you speak of the matter to anybody else?'

'Why should I? I wasn't interested.'

'May I take that as a reply in the negative, Mr Dickinson?'

'Take what you like.'

'Mr Maitland,' said Conroy again, more sharply this time.

'I should like a simple "yes" or "no" to my question,' Antony told the witness obligingly.

'What question?'

'Since you have so short a memory I will recapitulate. Did you mention Mr Franklin's coin collection to anybody else?'

'I did not.'

'Then the story couldn't have been spread through someone with whom you discussed it?'

'Certainly not. Mamie might have spoken about it, though, she found Henry's stories fascinating.'

'She has already assured us –'

'Then you can take it she didn't speak of the matter.'

'Thank you, Mr Dickinson, that's very helpful. Now let us turn to the cupboard in the hall at Kenyon Court.'

'The one under the stairs?'

'As far as I know that's the only one, isn't it?'

'Yes, it is. But what does it have to do with *this* case?'

'I'm asking the questions, Mr Dickinson. Have you had no conversation with your neighbours recently?'

'Naturally I have.'

'In that case I'm sure you know that Mrs Joyce Prior had the key to the cupboard, that it was used as an exchange point for the collections of money. It's an odd thing, incidentally, Mr Dickinson, that the two men whom I may call the collectors had such precise information about their victims.'

'Mr Maitland,' said Conroy.

'My lord?'

'Are you not straying from the point a little?'

Antony nearly said, it all depends what you think the point is, but he recollected himself in time and contented himself with, 'I beg your lordship's pardon.' But he had seen, or thought he had seen, the first startled question in the witness's eyes, and just for a moment he allowed himself to hope . . . 'That is a familiar story to you, Mr Dickinson, is it not?'

'You know it is.'

'Then I must ask you, did you ever see the two men concerned?'

'How should I know?'

'Perhaps because they would look out of place in Kenyon Court, and not like the sort of person likely to be visiting your neighbours.'

'I've frequently met people in the hall and on the stairs, of course —'

'I'm speaking of the hour between seven and eight in the evening, a weekday evening.'

'I never saw them.'

'One of the men is sitting in the court. Perhaps you would look around you and tell me if you recognise him.'

'I've already told you —'

'Please look around, Mr Dickinson.'

'Very well.' He did indeed let his eyes rove fleetingly around the crowded room before saying, 'I've already given you my answer, and I see nothing to make me change my mind.'

'Are you sure about that?'

'Of course I'm sure'

'Perhaps you would be kind enough to stand up, Mr Gray.'

There was an anxious pause before a whispered adjuration from the warder who accompanied him brought Alf to his feet. 'Do you recognise this man, Mr Dickinson?' Antony asked.

'I never saw him before.'

Antony let the silence lengthen a moment before he went on. 'In that case — thank you, Mr Gray, you may sit down — I must tell you that we are also interested in Mrs Prior's movements.'

'If you mean did I see her use her key to the cupboard, no I didn't.'

'According to your proof — your statement, Mr Dickinson — that forms part of my brief, you did see Mrs Prior leaving Kenyon Court once or twice in the morning with an attaché case.'

'Of course I did. We often left at the same time. And she was . . . I suppose you'd call her a career woman, naturally she'd be carrying a case.'

'You never saw her take it from the cupboard?'

'Of course not. She always waited until –'

'Until everyone was asleep, Mr Dickinson? Was that what you were going to say?'

'Only that I assume that's what she'd have done.'

Time was running out. Maitland was perfectly well aware that Mr Justice Conroy was growing impatient. 'How did Doctor Dickinson know that you were having an affair with Joyce Prior?' he asked abruptly.

Perhaps the suddenness of the question had its effect, perhaps the witness was already shaken. In either event he answered without apparent thought, 'Because she saw me leaving the Priors' flat one morning when Archie was away and I was supposed to be out of town.'

'So your wife told Mr Prior and there was to be a divorce. Did that please you?' (There was no time, at any moment the judge might stop this questioning. It could only have been sheer surprise that had kept him silent so long).

'Of course it didn't. The blasted women was talking about marriage . . . our marriage.'

'And you could hardly refuse, could you? She had a hold over you because you were providing the information on which the protection racket was based. You'd have had to divorce your wife?'

'I didn't want that, oh God, I didn't want that!'

'And so you killed Joyce Prior.' Question and answer had been coming breathlessly, as though neither man could get the story into the open fast enough. Now Rufus Dickinson seemed suddenly to realise that they were not alone, and oddly enough it was to the judge himself that he addressed his final words before pandemonium broke loose.

'There was nothing else I could do,' he said simply, and slowly released the convulsive grip he had taken on the rail in front of him, rather as though at the same time he were releasing his grip

186

on life.

But Antony had turned his eyes towards the press box and saw that it was empty, its occupants scrambling to be first out of the door.

I

'And what happened then?' asked Jenny breathlessly. It was tea-time that same afternoon, but Sir Nicholas – alerted by Bruce Halloran's legal grapevine – had come home some time since, and Antony had arrived just long enough ago to have completed his story of his examination of Rufus Dickinson. He smiled now at Jenny, but it was to his uncle that his answer was addressed.

'I expect you can imagine pretty well what happened,' he said.

'Mr Justice Conroy was not pleased with you,' Sir Nicholas hazarded.

'He was not!' Maitland closed his eyes for a moment in an effort of recollection. 'He said, "Mr Maitland, you've far exceeded the limits I set you, and if you had not taken me completely by surprise I should have stopped this very improper examination long since".'

'Meaning,' said Vera, 'he was interested himself in the outcome.'

'Yes, I think so. He then told the jury to disregard the witness's last remarks, and was about to confer with his clerk when who should appear in the well of the court but Sykes and Mayhew. Sykes asked the judge's permission to interrupt the proceedings for a moment, but it was all very seemly. They asked Dickinson to go with them, and he went.'

'But how on earth did Inspector Sykes get there?' asked Jenny. 'The case had nothing to do with him.'

'Chief Inspector,' Antony corrected her automatically, as he had been doing for years now, ever since Sykes's promotion. 'I saw him later and he said, "I thought there might be something in the wind, Mr Maitland, knowing you, so it might be worth my while to attend the court. I wonder you didn't notice me".'

'But you hadn't.'

'No, I was rather concentrated on what I was doing as a matter of fact. Sykes also said, in that admonitory way of his, "You were

188

treading on thin ice, I suppose you know that." But I don't think now I can be said to have harmed Archie Prior's defence, can I?'

'What had Sykes to say about that?' enquired his uncle.

'That Dickinson had seen his solicitor and made another statement, rather more comprehensive than the one he made in court. Also Alf Gray was now perfectly willing to identify him as the man who recruited him, obviously hoping it would be to his advantage. So Geoffrey started the wheels in motion to get Prior released.'

'And Jim Arnold?'

'Hawthorne and I weren't even put to the trouble of making our closing speeches. Conroy directed the jury that, though they had no alternative to finding the defendant guilty, they were at liberty to add that they felt his recent good record should be taken into account, and also the extreme provocation under which he had acted. Which they did, and Conroy sentenced him to one day in prison, which of course he has already served. So he's gone back to Fulham.'

'I see,' said Sir Nicholas thoughtfully.

'You needn't worry, Uncle Nick, I'm not going to badger you any more about getting him into Canada. Jimmy and Doris have decided to bring their families back to England. They're a strong-minded pair, they take after Mrs Arnold you know, and once they heard that Dad was in trouble –'

'Who told them, I wonder?'

'There's no mystery about it. I did.'

'So all that about using my influence –'

'It might have been necessary, but as it happens it isn't. In any case,' he added blandly, 'I thought it would do no harm for you to have something like that to occupy your mind, instead of concentrating your full attention on my activities.'

'I'm beginning to think,' said Sir Nicholas reflectively, 'that whatever Conroy found to say to you in court – and I cannot believe that you've reported on that fully – it was nowhere near sufficient.'

'Well, that's as maybe. And if you're wondering why he decided to be so lenient with Jim, I can only suggest that he'd noticed the stampede of reporters and knew quite well in what light my client was going to be presented to the public.'

189

'Could they report on it?' Jenny asked.

'Why not? It wasn't anything to do with the case in hand, as Conroy had pointed out, and Rufus Dickinson wasn't yet under arrest so no question of contempt of court could arise. Anyway, that was Conroy's motive, I think.'

'Cynical,' said Vera.

'That should please Uncle Nick, he's always complaining it's a quality I lack.'

'Still don't understand quite how you brought it off,' said Vera.

That brought a frown to Antony's brow. 'I didn't enjoy doing it,' he confessed. 'But it suddenly occurred to me, after I'd started examining Dickinson, that the thing that would upset Mamie Dickinson more than any other, the thing she'd never get over, would be if she herself was directly instrumental in bringing about her husband's downfall. So first of all I did my best to annoy him, and then I slipped in a few hints, which Conroy didn't like, and then I asked him a few point blank questions and he just went to pieces. He must have been a weak man underneath it all.'

'Have you seen Doctor Dickinson since he was arrested?' asked Jenny.

'Yes, for my sins. She's pretty broken up at the moment, of course, but she's a hard-working woman with a worthwhile job and I think she'll get over it. Besides' – he smiled suddenly with genuine amusement and Jenny and Vera exchanged a pleased glance – 'I hinted to her that Archie Prior would be pretty lonely and in need of cheering up. I wouldn't wonder –'

'This,' said Sir Nicholas, sitting up suddenly very straight, 'is more than I can bear. Jenny in the role of matchmaker I can tolerate if I must, it is the natureof women to meddle in this way. But you, Antony . . . words fail me!' he concluded.

'Nothing may come of it,' Antony pleaded. But for once his uncle had spoken with uncharacteristic inaccuracy. He still had a good deal to say.

II

However, when Sir Nicholas and his wife were alone together that

190

evening, Vera said, 'Can relax now, Nicholas, for a few months at least.'

'How do you make that out, my dear?'

'Told me yourself there's nothing in Antony's list this term to worry you. And as they'll be away throughout the Christmas vacation hé won't be able to become personally involved in anything that's going to come up in the Hilary term.'

'You're an optimist, Vera,' said Sir Nicholas. 'Besides, we don't know yet if they're going to America.'

'What do you bet?' asked Vera, and grinned unrepentantly when her husband shook his head at her. 'Meg,' she said, 'is a very persuasive woman.'